MEXICO

Steven R. James

MEXICO

Steven R. James Productions

Maine

For Alan

I want to thank both my editor Joanne and my partner in crime Alan for the hard work and hours that were put in editing this book. Their help was immeasurable and I could not have completed the book without them.

As the author and the person formatting the final draft for publication, I have the final say in edits and all content. If there are errors in the content of this book that is on me.

Steven R. James

Chapter 1

"EEEEEEEEEEEEEEEEEEEEEEEEEEEEEEEEEEEEEEEEEE
EEEEEEEEEEEEEEEEEEEEEEEEEEEEEEEEEEEEEEEEEE
EEEEEEEEEEEEEEEEEEEEEEEEEEEEEEEEEEEEEEEEEE
EEEEEEEEEEEEEEEEEEEEEEEEEEEEEEEEEEEEEEEEE!"
There was no mistaking the high-pitched squeals of excitement coming
from Michele Gibson and Patty Simmons as they stomped their feet and
jumped up and down with excitement. It was Sunday afternoon, June
19, 1985; both girls were in Michele's bedroom, still in their caps and
gowns, holding their high school diplomas and waving plane tickets in
the air. "OH, MY GAWD! I'm having a cow! This is wicked gnarly,
bodaciously bitchin' cowabunga awesome!" an overly excited Patty
screamed. Neither new high school graduate could contain their
excitement. Patty, who couldn't contain her emotions, continued her
ear-piercing screeching, "YAAAAAAAAAAAAAAAAAAAAAAY!"
Both girls were ecstatic as they continued jumping up and down like
children on Christmas morning. The girls couldn't contain themselves;
their minds were blown away with excitement and anticipation for the

upcoming adventure in Mexico. Sitting alone in the corner of Michele's bedroom in her pink bean bag chair was Michele's boyfriend Josh Baxter. Michele considered Josh nothing more than her boy toy. She did not like being in a relationship with her long-time childhood friend but did like getting high and having sex with him--since he didn't mind her kinky side and was willing to explore her deviant desires. Michele, being the hypersexual person (or what most would have called a nymphomaniac) that she was, considered his sexual prowess his only redeeming quality. Michele was an only child who always got what she wanted and always got her way. She was the epitome of a spoiled rotten brat because her father allowed it. Her mother was always on her dad about it and often tried to show him that one day he would regret raising her like this. She was never taught consequences, nor was she taught to take responsibility for herself and her actions. Because of that, she had a total disregard for others and no inhibitions, especially when it came to her fearless sexual promiscuity. That included what most considered, taboo. This was not the only reason she let Josh hang out with her. Living in a small Maine town, the dating pool was slim pickins' at best, not to mention, as Michele would say, "he grew some gnarly weed." Even though they had been friends since kindergarten, Michele had grown weary of the recent Miami Vice wannabe act and pathetic attempt at growing a mullet. She was going to tell him she just wanted to be friends. If he didn't like it, she would tell him to hit the bricks. After some thought, she decided to keep him around for two reasons: he had a green thumb, and he was the only guy in town she would sleep with. Michele and Josh had tried pot for the first time one Friday night and discovered the other effect pot had on them besides the high it gave them. They were hanging out by the pool at the Gibson residence. Michele was an attractive blond with a nice body and a beautiful face that didn't require makeup. The scant bikini she was wearing barely covered her large breasts and revealed her lady parts through the thin fabric. Josh was wearing a tight Speedo. For a skinny high school kid who never worked out, the Speedo looked good on him. As good as he looked in his Speedo, the one thing it didn't do was hide the erection he had. Between Michele's visible camel toe and the pot, Josh was feeling randy. Michele noticed this and right away started feeling that itch between her legs that her mother warned her about. It was not long before the kissing and touching started, leading to Michele making a man out of Josh. Today, Josh had that left-out feeling; he had his high school diploma in one hand and nothing in the other. Michele's father Sabastian, gave Michele an all-expense paid trip to Cancun, Mexico for graduation and was allowed to take Patty but not Josh. Michele and Josh thought they kept their sexual relationship a secret but living in a small central Maine town, word got around as to whose daughter was buying "the pill" from the local pharmacy. As hard as Sabastian tried, he could not ignore the rumors, nor could he ignore the fact that Princess was having sex with the weirdo kid from the hippie religious cult family. He never knew why Josh and Patty were allowed to hang out with anyone they wanted to. The other kids, the few kids that there were in what Patty's parents referred to as the "religious group", could not have friends outside the "church family". Sabastian hated Josh for soiling his Princess and loathed the thought that they were having sex on a regular basis. However, he did not want to upset his Princess, so he did his best to ignore what was going on. Sabastian had a bad habit of caving to every whim his little princess Michele had.

Downstairs in the formal parlor of the mini mansion that the Gibson's lived in, Sabastian and Kathleen were having another heated discussion, this time over the Mexico trip she forbade her husband to purchase. Kathleen, under no circumstances, wanted her daughter to go to Mexico unsupervised. She was angered by the fact that her husband went against her wishes and bought the trip for the girls, and was beyond furious over the situation, telling her husband that she could not believe he did this behind her back. Sabastian wasn't a perfect husband; he did have his faults, but never did he betray her trust like this. He was wrapped right around his daughter's little finger. She could do no wrong. It was not his Princess smoking pot by the pool, it was the weirdo kid. It was the weirdo kid's fault his Princess was on the pill. That is what Michele told her Daddy, and he always believed her. Just as it was, of course, the principal's fault when she almost didn't graduate. Or it was the fault of the administrators at the colleges she was rejected from, especially her top choice. Sabastian had to make a substantial donation towards the new high school library the town's school board was trying to raise funds for. He did this, and in return, he was able to get Princess's grades "adjusted" so she could graduate. Sabastian had to pull strings and call in a few favors, not to mention a bribe or two, to get Princess accepted to State University. Princess let him know that it was his fault for not getting her into a better college, which he apologized for and hoped a trip to Mexico would make it up to her. Michele owned her daddy, and she knew it. Her mother, however, was the disciplinarian. Kathleen, whom Michele referred to as "Queen Bitch", was nothing more than just an obstacle when she was trying to get her way. The heated discussion was quickly turning into a full-blown argument that was heard all the way upstairs by the three recent graduates. Josh and Patty could hear their voices. "What are they arguing about?" Josh asked. Patty, shrugging her shoulders replied, "I don't know, it's hard to make out what they are saying." Michele knew what they were arguing about. She heard this argument before. "Going to Mexico alone I forbid it! You can't buy her love! I am sick and tired of you giving her everything she wants! I can't believe you went behind my back and bought her this trip. It was her own damn fault she didn't get into a better school. You should have let her flunk and repeat her senior year. She needs to learn she isn't going to get her own way all the time. You created a monster with her!" Sabastian held his ground. "For Christ sakes Kathleen, she just turned eighteen! This is literally the last summer of her childhood. Let her have some fun before college! Always the prude, Kathleen!" She fired right back. "Always the prude! Remember what happened to Josh's mother on her last summer of her childhood! She is still on that fucking acid trip from Woodstock. Have you forgotten about that! Is that what you want for our daughter! Christ almighty you are her father, for once act like it!" Michele heard every word even if the other two didn't. She thought to herself, *I'm not going to let Queen Bitch ruin this trip.* In Mexico, she and Patty could party all they wanted and drink as much alcohol as they wanted. Both girls had just turned eighteen, the legal age in Mexico to consume alcohol and of course, it gave Michele a chance to sleep with other guys besides Josh. Michele said to her friends, "Let's change into our swimsuits and hang out by the pool." She was just using that as an excuse to go downstairs and try to break up the argument, making sure her trip did not get ruined. Both Josh and Michele started to undress. Michele and Josh had no issue changing in front of one another, but Patty was very uneasy about it. Patty has had a major crush on Josh since sixth grade. She even fantasized about what it would be like to marry Josh and have a family. When Michele told Patty about the night she and Josh had sex out by the pool, that should have upset Patty, but Patty idolized Michele so instead of being angry or jealous, she wanted to know every detail about what they did. She loved hearing all about her man crush and idol having sex. Patty was even trying to work up the nerve to bring up having a threesome. Other than some self-pleasuring, Patty was still a virgin. Even though she and Michele started on the pill together, she only had eyes for Josh. There were other guys who tried to get in Patty's pants, she would tell them she wanted a ring on the finger before she would give it up. If Patty was going to lose her virginity, it was going to be with Josh and no one else. She even considered doing a three-way with Michele and Josh if that is what it took to get Josh inside of her. The thought of him having an orgasm inside of her did more than make her feel a little moist. Patty was wanting to do whatever it took to have sex with Josh but just did not have the nerve to bring up the threesome. As uncomfortable as Patty was, she did strip down in front of Josh and asked, "Hey Josh, did you bring any weed so we can get baked by the pool?" Patty did that purposely; she wanted Josh to get a good look at her naked body but it didn't work as planned. Josh did not like the arguing that was going on downstairs. He played the role of cool stoner dude but that was just a false front; he would run from any confrontation. Josh really liked Patty a lot but was afraid to tell Michele he wanted to break up so he could ask Patty out. So, he put up with Michele. Josh was afraid of hurting Michele's feelings since they had been friends since kindergarten. He did not want to lose her as a friend and wasn't sure how she would take it. He was not afraid of Michele, but he also knew the tantrum she would throw if she didn't get her way. Josh looked up and liked what he saw. Patty was naked. She may not have had the D-cup breasts Michele had but she was just as hot as Michele in her own way. Even though Josh was checking Patty out, he didn't give Patty the reaction she was hoping for. Nonetheless, as uncomfortable as Patty was, she was glad to be naked in front of Josh.

The three quickly finished changing, and Michele hurried them along before Daddy caved to Queen Bitch. As Michele led the way downstairs, she was putting on a show. She bounced down the stairs and trotted into the parlor, "Oh, Daddy, I can't believe you did this!" with the overly dramatic enthusiasm she was known for. She wrapped her arms around her father's neck while jumping up and down as she continued with the same dramatics saying, "Daddy, I love you so, so much! Thank you, thank you, thank you!" This enraged Michele's mother, but Kathleen kept her cool. She knew what Michele was doing, and she would not give in. There was no way Michele was going to get her to lose her cool. Kathleen very sternly said, "You three go out and enjoy the pool. Mr. Gibson and I have got some talking to do." Michele immediately responded. "OH, mother please! We are eighteen now and responsible adults, don't be a prude." Again, keeping her cool, Kathleen looked at her husband with her daughter's arms still draped around his neck, and said to Sabastian, "We will continue this conversation later," leaving the four of them in the parlor.

Chapter 2

A shiny, red, 1987, Pontiac Fiero sat idling on a side road, in the darkness of night. The young female driver could not hear a single vehicle on State Road 41. Known as the Tamiami Trail, it runs down the Gulf of Mexico side of Florida from the Georgia state line, across the Everglades and into Miami on the Atlantic Ocean side of the Florida Peninsula. The area where the young female driver decided to stop was mostly desolate at night because this section of the road runs through the deepest parts of the Everglades. She decided to pull off the highway by turning down one of the access roads that the Everglades Park Rangers use. She wanted to be completely out of sight. She chose a desolate section because she did not want to risk being disturbed by another passing motorist trying to be a good Samaritan, stopping to ask if she needed help or was having car trouble. The area she chose was just that: desolate. She had driven about a hundred yards down the well-packed limestone road. The night air was heavy with humidity, and in the darkness, she could barely see the sawgrass on each side swaying in the slight breeze, which provided little relief from the steamy subtropical climate. The sawgrass became taller the further she drove down this section of the Tamiami Trail called Alligator Alley. The sugar-sand soil that Florida is known for gave way to the richer, swampier soil in which the sawgrass thrived. Next to her on the passenger seat was a pad of paper, a pen, and her purse, which contained an almost empty bottle of tequila, a bottle of vodka, several vials of cocaine, and some sleeping pills. The sleeping pills were for those nights when her mind wouldn't stop racing from the pent-up anxiety she refused to acknowledge. She sat there for several minutes in the dark just staring out the windshield into the blackness that surrounded her. The past two and a half months did not go as planned. She thought she had won, she thought she had gotten her power back, she thought she was in control, but most of all she thought her family, especially her father, would be proud of her for winning. She sat there behind the wheel with the engine idling and lights off, staring out the windshield into the darkness of the swamp, wracking her brain trying to figure out where, when, how, and why it all went wrong. She had driven through every state on the east side of the Mississippi trying to figure this out and what to do next. She was both physically and mentally exhausted, at a loss of trying to find answers. She was thinking that this road trip, wandering aimlessly through the East Coast states, would provide the answers she so desperately sought and maybe even find herself. The other reason she stopped and pulled off the road was simply because she had to pee. Feeling the pressure growing in her bladder, she reached over to the glove compartment to retrieve some napkins from the growing collection. There was an endless supply of napkins from fast-food drive-thrus she had been frequenting as of late. When she opened the door to the glove compartment, the thirty-eight-caliber handgun she bought from that creepy redneck in Kentucky fell out and onto the passenger side floor. She had to pee so badly; she just left the gun there, shut the engine and got out of the car. She barely got her panties down before she started peeing as she leaned against the small car trying to squat so she would not splash herself. She was grateful for the napkins; drip drying just was not her thing. Once her bladder was empty again, her panties back on and her Daisy Dukes buttoned back up, she opened the car door to get back in when she heard this ungodly hiss from the front of the car. At first, she thought one of her tires must somehow have gotten punctured. Then she heard the low growl that followed the hissing sound. Startled by this and now knowing it wasn't a tire, she jumped back into her car and threw the headlights on, revealing the fifteen-foot-long snapping-jawed reptile. Having never seen an alligator before was scary enough, but with the red beady eyes glaring back in the headlights, it made it even scarier. The bony spikes protruding from its scaly back gave it a dinosaur-like look. Its jagged teeth and jaw were snapping, and that short lunge forward after each snap terrified her. Not thinking clearly and forgetting about the handgun on the passenger side floor, she thrust both her hands onto the center of the steering wheel, blasting the horn at the hideous beast. With a long blast followed by short bursts from the horn, the reptilian beast stopped: the stare down began. Both the young woman and the beast were locked in a battle of wills. Who would flinch first was the game they were playing. Sitting there for only a few minutes, which seemed like an eternity, she realized the gun was within her reach. Having never fired a gun before, the only real hope she had was to scare the beast off. She leaned over with eyes still locked on the massive beast and picked up the gun. She thought it was better to leave the car door closed and just roll down the window. She stuck her hand with the gun in it out the window, using her thumb to pull the hammer back, and listened for the second click like the toothless wonder who sold her the gun told her to do. He was a man she would never forget because the stench of his body odor made it smell like he hadn't bathed since Nixon resigned. She thought he smelled like the contents of a septic tank, and the stained overalls he wore looked like they were never laundered. She took aim at the beast. Just as she had the gun aimed, it suddenly, with a terrifying lunge, came at her with lightning speed. It was as if the beast knew the imminent danger he was in. It let out a ferocious hiss, causing the young woman to scream and drop the gun. The gun landed next to the car. The impact of hitting the hard, packed limestone road caused the hammer to trigger the gun, wildly firing a bullet into the sawgrass. The loud firecracker-type noise caused the enormous gator to stop its forward attack and bolt off into the sawgrass on the opposite side of the car. A few seconds later, she heard the gator splashing down into the swampy waters, and it was gone faster than it appeared. Taking several minutes to catch her breath and get her wits about her after the horrific ordeal, she opened the car door, reached down, and picked up the gun. She placed the gun on her lap and reached over to the passenger seat, grabbing the open bottle of tequila out of her oversized bag. She opened the bottle, taking the last few big gulps of what was left of the fiery liquid, in hopes the alcohol would help calm her down. She gasped for air and coughed from the burn of the 80-proof liquid and she took the pad of paper and pen in hand. Using the steering wheel to support the pad so she could write, she drew in a deep breath before taking pen to paper. She started writing, "This is my side of it.

Chapter 3

Michele and Patty were lying on the lounge chairs by the poolside in their scant bikinis that left little to the imagination. Josh was at the far end of the pool, floating on a pool float. He was lying face down, facing the opposite direction from the girls. He needed to zone out and reground himself. The arguing and tension between Michele's parents brought out his anxiety. Josh suffers from conflict phobia; it never seems to matter whether it is a direct confrontation or his witnessing a confrontation up close that seems to trigger his anxiety, causing a flight response and panic attack. Although rarely visible on the outside, he is a total train wreck mentally when his phobia rears its ugly head. He found that smoking pot helps tremendously when he needs to calm himself. Since Michele's parents were within smelling distance, smoking a bong was out of the question. Just being out of earshot of everyone, including Patty and Michele, was a way he could ground himself. This was going to have to do since it was his only option. Every time Michele looked in his direction, all she could see was the back of his head. She hated that poor excuse for a mullet and had no issue telling

Patty that. Patty kept it to herself that she disagreed with her about the mullet and Josh. She thought he was hot and wanted him in the worst way. Michele turned back to Patty and started talking about the Mexico trip. She told Patty, or more like threatened Patty, to keep the plans she was about to lay out to herself. She told her friend she was going to find out what it was like to have sex with someone besides Josh. Michele was planning on partying with as many guys as she could to try and satisfy her never-ending sexual appetite. She was frustrated with this one-stoplight town and its lack of decent guys. Most guys in this central Maine town were more interested in hunting, fishing, and how high they could lift the suspension on that shit box of a pick-up truck they had, so they could put on monster mud tires. Michele never got the allure of tires that were taller than she was. That was the one thing about Josh she did like; he never saw the point of those lifted monster-tire trucks. But then again, getting laid in his AMC Pacer was no prize either. She felt like she was having sex in a fishbowl. Their lack of personal hygiene and nonexistent use of a toothbrush made guys in this town a total turn-off. She swore that the three of them were the only ones in their high school who knew what soap was and how to use it. As Patty sat listening intently to Michele's plans for their trip, Michele asked Patty if she was going to finally have sex and put the prescription for the pill to good use. Right after Josh and Michele had sex for the first time, Michele talked Patty into going on the pill together. She told Patty that losing her virginity totally rocked her world. Her first orgasm was much more than she ever imagined an orgasm could be. She said to

Patty that it was explosive and came in waves that shuddered her whole body. She said she could feel Josh cum inside her. The whole experience was intense. The way she felt afterwards was better than the high she got from the pot. Michele knew she was lucky that she did not get pregnant that night. Knowing that she needed to do something to prevent an unwanted pregnancy, since Josh could not put a condom on to save his life, she decided to go on the pill. To appease Michele, Patty agreed and went on the pill with her. Patty was surprised her mother had agreed to her going on the pill. Patty would learn later that her mother wished she had gone on the pill when she was in high school. She took part in the whole free love movement of the sixties and got pregnant with Patty by her father at their senior prom. Remembering how teenagers were, Patty's mom was quick to agree when Patty said she and Michele wanted to go on the pill together. Michele's mother agreed for the same reason. Josh turned his head and saw the girls deeply engaged in conversation. Usually, the anxiety attacks lasted no more than fifteen minutes. This anxiety attack was relentless; it held a tight and firm grip on him. The way the girls were talking and keeping their voices low added to his panic. His mind was racing with all kinds of worries. *Were they making fun of him when he got naked in front of them? Was Michele giving Patty hell because she stared at his naked body?* His overthinking of the situation was getting the best of him. He could not settle himself and needed to get high. Josh got out of the pool and told the girls his parents were taking him out for a graduation dinner, and he had to leave. This was not a lie; his parents were taking him out, however, the dinner reservations were for eight that evening at Calvaries in Augusta. This was where all the state lawmakers would go. It was the finest restaurant around without having to drive to Old Port or Bangor. It was just four o'clock in the afternoon with plenty of time to hang out with his friends. Regardless, this was the excuse he needed to leave. He quickly rounded up his clothes and took off to do what he needed to do.

As soon as Josh was gone, Michele turned to Patty and continued the conversation about her plans. Patty loved the sounds of everything except the cheating on Josh part. Patty, being secretly in love with Josh, felt bad about that part. Patty did not want to ruin her trip to Mexico and was hoping the trip would be the thing to get them to break up. With Patty and Josh both being accepted into Mercy College, and Michele going to State College this fall, she was hoping the trip would get those two to break up, then she could make her move. Even though that was wishful dreaming on her part, it did give her hope and put at ease the bad feelings about the plans Michele had for Mexico. She secretly vowed to remain a virgin for Josh.

Chapter 4

The small Air Canada shuttle that departed Bangor International Airport carrying the two female passengers who were headed to Mexico for a trip of a lifetime, gently touched down in Quebec, Canada. Michele had been containing her excitement and didn't talk much on the short flight. She was excited, not because they were on their way to the resort town of Cancun, Mexico, but because she was going to be spending some time with her cousin Lily, too. Lily and Michele were remarkably close and visited often. Having a pilot in the family made travel easy, and the cost of a ticket was less than a tank of gasoline. Ever since Michele's first solo visit to Quebec, the girls slept in Lily's room. Lily's mother would set up the fold-a-bed for Michele. The girls would mess up the sheets on the fold-a-bed then climb into Lily's bed together. When the girls turned thirteen and started maturing into womanhood, Lily told Michele during one of their "girl talk sessions" about her nymphomania. Michele had been experiencing her own uncontrollable urges, which were caused by the surge of hormones that was awakening her own insatiable sexual appetite since puberty had struck. Hearing that her cousin was experiencing the same thing brought a sense of relief, knowing she wasn't some sort of freak. During their girl talk session, Lily asked Michele if she wanted to play the game truth or dare, telling Michele she could go first if she said yes. Michele had not played truth or dare before, but there was a certain excitement she felt about the game. Michele didn't even ask Lily truth or dare she just asked Lily if she had kissed a guy. Lily had kissed a few guys and had gone all the way with one of them, too, which she admitted to but not for extra credit. It was because Lily was setting Michele up. Michele couldn't believe it when she found out Lily had sex and wanted to know all about it, but Lily said, "No, my turn," and asked Michele if she had kissed a boy yet. Not wanting to admit that she hadn't kissed a boy and was still a year away from making a man out of Josh, Michele said, "Like duhhh! of course I have. I even let him touch my boob." Lily was excited for her cousin and did what teenage girls do; she let out a squeal and hugged her cousin. Letting go of Michele, Lily said, "Okay, okay, my turn again. Have you ever kissed a girl?" was Lily's question, which got an "EWWWW! NO!" for a reply. Michele then asked Lily her truth or dare question, "Have you ever kissed a girl." Lily replied no but there is always a first time for everything." Lily leaned in and started kissing her cousin. At first, Michele did not like the kiss and kept her mouth closed but that didn't last as Michele could feel herself getting aroused. Michele never experienced such an arousal before relaxing her jaw and allowing Lily to slide her tongue into her mouth. Michele was so eager to explore more that she let herself go and let her hypersexuality take over, allowing things to take their course. It was not long before the girls were pleasuring one another and lip-locked in sexual passion. That was the night Michele experienced her first unforgettable orgasm. It was on that visit that Michele allowed Lily to become her mentor, giving into her newly found deviant side. Lily told Michele that having sex, even if others considered it taboo, was nothing for her to be ashamed of. Michele thought of it like Lily gave her permission; the permission she needed to explore her sexual prowess. That night, Lily taught Michele that acting on her sexual desires and letting go of all her inhibitions was okay. Quebec has a larger population of males than the area Michele lived in, making it easy for Lily to be more experienced with men than Michele was. The fact that the women on Michele's maternal side were well-endowed when it came to their breast size, the natural symmetry of their facial features, and the hourglass shape that filled out the "little black dress" had most men eager to make their acquaintance. Lily took full advantage of that. She would soon be teaching Michele the skills that Michele would be using on her soon-to-be boyfriend, Josh Baxter. From that night on, whenever Michele visited, sleeping together was no longer the innocent thing it once was.

Lily's father is employed as an airline pilot with Air Canada, a company known for giving their employees generous job perks. The Airline's employees were given deep discounts to the numerous resort destinations that Air Canada would fly to. It was Lily's father whom Sabastian went through to book the trip for the girls. Michele and her cousin were the same age and despite the distance, Lily's father suggested the brief visit as part of the trip since they were going to need a connecting flight. Michele's cousin was going to be living abroad and studying in Europe come the fall, so the stopover was a chance to see one another before Lily headed to Europe. Lily is the daughter of Kathleen Gibson's younger sister, Emily. Michele and Lily were, as you might say, "Apples that didn't fall far from the tree." Michele's mother, being aware of her daughter's hypersexuality, knew that her daughter was just like her. Kathleen was trying to protect Michele from the mistakes she and Emily made at that age. Kathleen kept hidden from her daughter and husband that she had contracted the clap in high school after she and Emily got caught up in the free love movement that was taking the hippie counterculture of the 1960's by storm. Kathleen and Emily were not shy about being part of the movement, but unlike Emily, Kathleen felt that condoms ruined the experience. Kathleen chose the pill over condoms as birth control and found out the hard way that the pill did not protect her from STDs nor was the pill as effective as a condom if you missed taking it even briefly. Kathleen had contracted the clap and was afraid to tell her parents about the STD. Out of fear, Kathleen allowed the STD to go untreated, causing sepsis. The sepsis led to her having a miscarriage. This was something she never told her high school sweetheart, Sabastian Gibson, about. It wasn't Sabastian who got Kathleen pregnant, and it was someone else besides the baby's father that gave her the clap. Kathleen did not want Sabastian to find out, and by the grace of God, Sabastian never did. It was a secret Kathleen would end up taking to the grave. Kathleen's mother told her she got lucky that the infection had cleared up in a few short weeks without any long-term complications. Unlike most infections, it can take months to clear and can cause sterility. Kathleen would never tell her daughter the reason she was so strict, mostly out of shame.

At the arrival gate, the girls greeted one another, engaging in typical high-pitched, obnoxious teenage girl screams, "Oh my God it's so gnarly to see you!" accompanied by big hugs. After introducing Patty to Lily, they quickly shuffled off to baggage claim so they could get to Lily's house, drop off the bags, and then hit the bars. The legal drinking age in the Quebec Province is eighteen, and the girls wanted to start partying right away, and party they did. The three of them started bar hopping, jumping around to random bars, downing shots of tequila at one bar, then shots of vodka at another. Around ten that night, they hit the sixth and final bar in the downtown district. The bar they stopped at was Bronco Billy's Tavern. Bronco Billy's was a western-themed bar that featured local bands who played everything from old school country music to rock and roll. Tonight, the band that was booked was your typical eighties hair band. Clad in tight spandex, high top sneakers, tight tee shirts and big hair, the band was trying to be the next Bon Jovi or Motley Crew. They took notice of the girls right away, sending a few complimentary rounds of vodka shots to their table. When the drinks arrived, the waitress told the girls who sent the shots over to them and the three of them shouted, "WOOOOOO! Partying like a Rock Star!" They downed the shots and immediately ordered another round. The Band took their final break of the night. Normally, the entire band would head out back to snort a line or spark up a joint. This time, the singer and drummer, who were twin brothers, approached the table the girls were at while the rest of the band went out back. The tables in the bar were round, and the drummer took a seat in between Patty and Michele, and the singer sat between Michele and Lily. They introduced themselves as Mark and Matt Gunner. They were in their mid-twenties and possessed the typical blonde hair blue-eyed good looks that had all three girls ogling. The twins knew they were being ogled over; each slid a hand under the table and started rubbing the inner thigh of each girl. Michele, having a guy on each side of her, gently spread her legs to accommodate a hand from each of the twins. Michele and Lily leaned in to whisper in the ears of the twins, telling them they were not wearing any panties. The twins were quick to see if it was true. To their delight, it was true. Michele had a twin on each side of her, and she made sure each twin got a feel of what she had to offer. Even though Patty had on her Jordache jeans, she did enjoy the hand massage she was getting, and glad she wore a panty liner. The rest of the band returned to the stage and signaled to the twins to join them for the last set of the night. The twins ordered more rounds of vodka shots for the girls and told all three to hang out after the show.

The girls met the twins out in the parking lot by the van they drove. The rest of the band had already taken off with the rented cargo van in which they hauled equipment. Patty had passed out in the back of Lily's car; the final shot of vodka at last call was too much for her. Matt slid the side door of the van open, exposing the queen-sized mattress on the floor of the van. The girls needed no coaxing. They hopped right in and sat next to one another on the mattress with their legs spread exposing themselves to Mark and Matt. Lily was the one who asked the guys if they knew how to use their tongue. Nodding in unison, and with huge grins on their faces, both said, "Oh yeah we do." They quickly got in the van, slid the door closed and started right in on pleasuring the girl's feminine divine. Michele and Lily lay back and let the guys do their thing. Lily rolled her head to her side to face her cousin, and reaching down, she took Michele by the hand. Michele rolled her head to face her cousin and took her hand. Staring one another in the eye Lily leaned in and started kissing her cousin. Michele relaxed and let her slide her tongue into her mouth and allowed herself to get lost in the ecstasy of the moment. The brothers came up for air and saw the girls kissing. Matt said, "That's so fucking hot," before sliding their spandex off, releasing the pressure their erections were creating, and getting themselves in position so they could slide into each one of the girls. The kissing between the girls intensified as the guys thrust themselves inside of them harder and harder until finally Mark shouted, "OH God I'm busting a nut!" Both Lily and Michele could not hold back their orgasms. Their bodies began to shudder as they arched their backs up, thrusting their hips into the guy's midsections. Matt followed suit, yelling, "OH GOD! OH GOD!" From the outside of the van, you could hear the four of them getting off at the same time with the van rocking back and forth on its squeaking shocks and springs. Patty lay passed out, oblivious to the orgy happening in the van parked right next to her in the dimly lit alley behind the bar.

Later that night, the girls led a still semi-comatose Patty to the rec-room sofa, where she would spend the rest of the night sleeping off the alcohol she consumed. The cousins went up to Lily's bedroom and with tonight being no different than any other, they got in bed together. They engaged in a little pillow talk about what they did with the guys. Michele told Lily how great Matt was before he slid himself into her, but admitted she liked it better when Lily did it to her. Lily was quick to agree. Mark was great, but Michele was much better at it. The girls rolled over towards one another, each kissing the other good night. Michele pulled her cousin closer, so their naked breasts were pressing together, nipple to nipple. She reached down so she could pleasure her cousin. Lily responded by returning the favor. The girls kissed while bringing one another to their second orgasms of the night. Good looks and sexual deviancy ran in their family, and both girls were not afraid to push the limits of their desires. It's who they were.

Chapter 5

The following morning the three girls stopped for breakfast on their way to the airport. The connecting flight to Mexico didn't leave till noon, leaving plenty of time for breakfast at Lily's favorite spot. Scrambles is a small bistro-style breakfast-only diner in the heart of downtown Quebec. The three sat in a booth at the far end of the diner. Lily and Michele were seated across from one another, sipping coffee and engaging in light chit chat. Patty was no stranger to alcohol, but she was more a Boones Farm or Bartles and Jaymes wine cooler drinker versus the vodka and tequila shot type. Every time she would open a Bartles and Jaymes wine cooler, Josh would say, "Thank you for your support!" Patty would reply, "You're welcome." They would start laughing and Michele would roll her eyes in disgust at the two of them. Patty didn't take part in the conversation; her head was pounding, and her stomach was still doing flip-flops. It was all she could do to hold down the mug of coffee she drank. The vodka and tequila shots proved to be too much. She thought, *how could those two party like that and not be hungover like she was?* The waitress arrived with three plates of eggs, toast, two different fried breakfast meats, and a side of corned beef hash. The mere sight and smell of all this food caused Patty to start dry heaving and quickly made a beeline to the ladies' room. Her morning coffee was about to make an exit through the entrance. With Patty gone, Michele said to Lily, "Last night in the van was awesome." Lily told Michele she loved that the guys didn't use condoms. She hates the feel of them. Michele replied, "I didn't know you were on the pill too till last night." Lily said she wasn't on the pill because she didn't like the health risks of being on the pill. Lily said, "It's Canada and abortions are free." She told Michele about an underground abortion clinic that will do unrestricted abortions. She told Michele the people who run it are radicalized activists who are pushing Canada to remove all the restrictions on abortions. Lily had had three different abortions there since becoming sexually active. She told Michele that they do not report the abortion, ask for ID, or require parental consent. Michele asked Lily if there was a limit on how many abortions a woman could have before it causes health issues. She also asked her cousin if she felt bad about aborting the baby. Lily said that was the awesome part that you could have as many as you want, and the health risks were a lot less and almost non-existent compared to the pill. Then Lily said, "About feeling bad." She stopped there so she could lean in and lower her voice so only Michele could hear the next part, "It's just an embryo, it's not like it's a real baby." Michele never thought of it that way and admitted to herself that Lily is right. These are the same words Michele will be using on someone in the not so distance future. Lily leaned back into her seat after she said that and started eating her breakfast just as Patty was headed back over to the booth. Patty, feeling much better now, started to nibble at her eggs. Making sure she could hold food down, and feeling confident that she could, she made quick work of the plate that was in front of her. The girls finished breakfast, and it was off to a couple of boutiques for shopping then to the airport.

Chapter 6

Evan Mills was your typical brawny and ruggedly handsome farm boy. He stood about six feet tall and outgrew his boyish good looks at a young age. At fourteen he had already started to take on the features that gave him his ruggedly handsome good looks. His chiseled jawline only added to that almost perfect symmetry to his face. Evan grew up on a cattle farm in Myakka City, located east of Sarasota. His father was a very strict Southern Baptist minister invoking the fear of God in Evan at an early age. Because of his up bringing, Evan steered clear of drugs and alcohol. Even though he had the girls throwing themselves at him in both high school and college, he remained a virgin due to his hellfire and brimstone upbringing, making sex out of wedlock, forbidden. Evan loved being outdoors and tending to the livestock and large gardens on the ranch his parents owned. As much as Evan loved being on the ranch, he adored the Everglades and the wildlife that called the Everglades home. He strongly believed protecting the Everglades ecosystem was his true calling in life. Evan attended USF and graduated in 1985 with a bachelor's degree in environmental science and a minor in wildlife management. Knowing his true calling in life was to protect Florida's Everglades, he was quick to enter a graduate program studying how humans and now the invasive species of pythons were impacting the ecosystem and native wildlife. Evan was out doing his nightly routine of tracking and recording the native wildlife population of the Florida Everglades, when he heard a single gunshot go off. By how loud the sound was, he figured whoever shot the gun was close by. Thinking it may be a poacher, he felt the need to check things out.

The young female driver could see headlights off in the distance getting closer. Knowing she could get in a boatload of trouble, she quickly stashed the gun under her seat, threw her pen and pad of paper with "This is my side of it" written on the first line, and closed the zipper on her bag. She got everything secured and out of sight just as the Chevy K10 pickup truck with the blinding high beams still on, stopped in front of her. Evan opened the driver's door of the pickup and stepped out. He was standing with the door open using the door as a shield to protect him and left the engine running in case he needed a quick getaway. Shouting to the person in the small red car that was in front of him, he identified himself. After identifying himself, he asked if the driver was OK, he had heard a gunshot. With a quick spray of Binaca to get the smell of tequila off her breath, the young woman got out of the car with an arm raised to shield her eyes from the bright headlights. When Evan saw the young woman was alone, he reached in and turned off his high beams, leaving the headlights on. The young woman wanted nothing more than to get rid of this guy so she could get back to what she was doing. As he approached her, and her eyes adjusted to the headlights, she could see who she was talking to. Right away she noticed his rugged good looks and the way his uniform fitted his well-sculptured body. Immediately she thought the dry spell was over. This is definitely a guy she would love to slide her panties off for, so he could do her right there on the hood of her car. That thought was quickly gone as they were now face-to-face, and she got a weird feeling. Even though he gave her an eerie feeling, she wasn't afraid of him, nor did she feel he was there to cause her harm, which was a feeling she knew all too well. This was different and she immediately lost all sexual interest in him. She wasn't intimidated by him, she felt a warm sense of peace in his presence. Even so, she felt that urge to get rid of him quickly. Evan told her he was doing research on the next access road over and repeated that he had heard a gunshot. The young woman, who was good at thinking on her feet, said, "No that was my car backfiring." She told Evan that she stopped to rest a bit. She said that she got out of her car to get her tote bag that was in the luggage compartment. She somehow felt telling him she got out to pee wasn't a good idea. When she was getting back in the car, she heard something hissing and growling. She told him in a panic, she jumped into the car, threw her headlights on and saw a freaking real live dinosaur. She said in her panic of trying to start the car so she could get away, she must have flooded the engine, causing the backfire. She was playing the part of the poor damsel in distress so well that she was convinced Evan bought her story hook, line, and sinker. Evan smiled because he knew she was talking about Big Al, the largest and oldest gator in that area. He was a tough one too. Evan witnessed a battle between Big Al and a python that was the same size as Big Al lengthwise. It was a short battle as Big Al easily won and swallowed the snake in one big gulp. He left that detail out when he told the young woman it was Big Al she saw. Evan told her the gator had scared him on several occasions too. Trying to make polite and light conversation, he told her how he had gotten used to Big Al, especially after he tranquilized him for tagging. And he was a hard gator to tranquilize too. Evan told her how he was kneeling over the gator with a knee on each side, and its head lifted in both hands, so the gator's head was at the same height as Evan's. Even with the gator's mouth taped shut and thinking he used enough tranquilizer on the gator, the gator started doing the death roll sending both Evan and the gator into the water. Luckily, Evan was able to get away from the gator and scramble up the embankment to grab the tranquilizer gun and hit the gator with another dart before it took off with its mouth still taped closed. Evan was glad the gator didn't get away with its mouth taped closed; he was defenseless and could starve to death. The young woman was less than impressed with the story and wanted him to go. Evan could sense she was just being polite by not interrupting his story. He returned the politeness by not telling her he didn't believe her because of the heavy humidity in the Florida air, the odor of gun powder was still lingering. He did tell her that he was going to check to make sure Big Al was gone. He grabbed his hand-held floodlight out of his pickup truck and started checking the area the gator took off to. He was looking for a blood trail to see if she shot the gator. As Evan leaned forward, looking into the sawgrass the young woman noticed just how well his uniform pants accentuated his ass. Normally this would get her aroused and she would get that tingle and urge between her legs. But it wasn't happening, she still felt nothing and just wanted him to leave. After finding no blood, Evan did a quick sweep with the light on the ground and into the sawgrass and found a small patch of fallen sawgrass from the bullet's path. Knowing she hadn't hit the gator, Evan figured he should just leave; he did believe the part of the story where she was just resting. Evan told her she was safe; the gator is most likely a good mile or so away by now and won't be back. She thanked Evan for making sure she was safe. She was going to finish resting, then be on her way. She said she was sorry that she pulled him away from his research as she was walking back to get in her car. Evan knew when he wasn't wanted and was happy to leave and get back to his research. As he was backing away, he had a feeling they would be meeting again sooner rather than later. After settling back in her car, the young woman placed the pad of paper on her lap. She got the bottle of vodka out of her bag and took a few good swigs of the fiery liquid. She capped the bottle and placed it back in her bag, then sat back and tried to think about what to write and who to write the note to. It wasn't long before the relaxing effects of the liquid took over, causing her to drift off into restless sleep.

Chapter 7

The nonstop flight from Quebec to Mexico left right on time. The flight was smooth with no turbulence, touching down and pulling up to the gate as scheduled. The uneventful flight gave Patty a chance to sleep off the hangover, albeit slight compared to that morning, but still lingering. The girls departed the plane filled with excitement for the freedom they would have from their parents while in Mexico. They quickly made their way to the baggage claim to gather their luggage. Once outside, Michele started looking for their driver. Her uncle had arranged for him to pick them up and take them safely to the resort.

Amburo was standing on the sidewalk in front of the shiny black Lincoln Town Car the resort used to pick their guests up as they arrived at the airport. Amburo was standing about fifty feet or so from the exit doors of the baggage claim area. Amburo, whose full name was Amburo Aaden Omar, is a refugee from the violence in Somalia. He and his mother had fled the war-torn country of Somalia after their village was seized by the warlords who destroyed and burned the homes of the villagers to the ground. The ruthless, violent warlords of the corrupt

Government of Somalia were trying to destroy the resistance fighters. There were times they would send soldiers in to attack the defenseless villagers. The soldiers were known for the terrorizing tactics they used on the innocent, to send profane messages to the resistance. Attacking villages like the one Amburo and his mother lived in, sent a clear message to the villagers: that aligning themselves with the resistance movement would cause a torturous death to all who resisted. This was a show of the strength and dominance they had over the resistance. Amburo and his mother were able to flee Somalia through the resistance movement and find refuge in Mexico, where they were granted asylum and employment at a resort, one day hoping to apply for a permanent residence visa. Although they were able to physically be removed from that violence, their escape could not remove the deep-rooted trauma and emotional scars that would never heal from the monstrous acts and unspeakable horrors they experienced. The soldiers brutalized Amburo and his mother consistently over the course of several weeks before burning down their small hut along with what little possessions they owned. Amburo has had the same night terror ever since that first night the soldiers broke down the already weaken

ed entrance door to their tiny and meager home. His night terror would begin with the soldiers kicking in the front door and storming into their home. The soldiers would create a chaos that would cause enough confusion that Amburo and his mother were unable to comprehend what was happening. While in that numb state of mind, they easily overpowered the young Amburo who was just shy of puberty. They tied him to the dining table chair and gagged his mouth so he couldn't scream. Once gagged, each soldier took their turn beating him. Some would land a fist in the face; others would land a fist in his midsection. One of the fists to the midsection struck him directly in the stomach causing him to vomit his dinner up. Because the gag was tied so tightly, the vomit had no place to go causing Amburo to choke on the regurgitated contents from his stomach. His only option was to try and swallow the vomit so he could breathe again. One of the soldiers pulled Amburo's head back and forced his eyes open so he could insert an eye speculum into his eyelids. When they finished, they pushed the chair towards the table they had his mother tied to. With his eyes forced open and the rancid taste of stomach acid and the chunks of undigested food he couldn't swallow, Amburo was forced to watch the monstrous acts the soldiers would perform on his mother. His mother was bent over face down on the table. Her legs were spread apart and tied to each table leg. Her dress was lifted over her head and her undergarments were torn off, exposing her completely. Each one of her arms was tied to a table leg at the other end as her head hung down over the edge of the table, facing down. The soldiers had gagged her using an O-ring style gag, leaving her mouth wide open and exposed. Although the soldiers took turns pounding their fists into his mother's back and kidney area. The beating was not as severe as the beating they gave Amburo. They had other plans for his mother. There were four soldiers at the end of the table where her backside was exposed, and two at her head. Amburo was forced to watch the ungodly way the soldiers violated his mother.

Amburo could not close his eyes or turn away from the unspeakable acts the depraved soldiers did with their rifles to his mother. One of the soldiers laughed and told Amburo it was his love gun as he continued the assault on her, which was nothing short of blasphemy. The other soldiers laughed as the helpless Amburo watched. The two soldiers at the other end of the table slapped their victim several times across the face, then grabbed her by the hair, lifting her head, so her face was at crotch level. One soldier held her head up by her hair. Using his other hand, he steadied her head so she could not turn away. The second soldier slid his pants to his knees and slid himself into her mouth till she choked. Her head was forcibly held in place while tears streamed down her cheeks, as he performed this heinous act. The soldier who was using the barrel of his rifle inside her removed the barrel so that the other soldiers could commit other atrocities to her as well. The soldier in command of his troops was forcing Amburo to watch as his soldiers brutally raped his mother. The other soldiers cheered as the anger and rage grew inside Amburo. There was nothing he or his mother could do. He was just a child, being overpowered by grown men. All he could do was watch the savagery while the soldiers laughed and taunted him. The two soldiers who were pleasuring themselves in her mouth were forcing her gag reflexes to react, leading to uncontrollable dry heaving. Each dry heave felt like a gut punch as she choked. When they finished, they let her head drop down. She had no strength; her head just dangled as her saliva and the soldier's bodily fluids ran from her mouth and pooled on the floor below. When the other soldiers were done committing their unholy acts on the helpless woman, the commander and largest of the soldiers, picked Amburo up while still tied to the chair. He carried Amburo, chair and all, to the other end of the table positioning him so he could see his mother's backside. The soldier boisterously said "Hey! the boy wants some of momma too!" as he shoved Amburo's face into his mother. The commander smeared Amburo's face into the remnants of his mother's blood, and the soldier's bodily fluids. After smearing the aftermath of the brutal rape onto the boy's face, he pulled Amburo back, lifting him, chair and all, so they were face to face. Amburo was wailing in horror and screaming for them to stop through the gag. The soldier hollered, "Why are you crying, don't you love your momma? Here's something you can cry over!" he said as he was hurled the still tied Amburo across the room and headfirst into the far wall knocking the boy out cold. The soldiers cut Amburo's mother free and, as before, the commander kicked the table over, sending Amburo's mother sprawling hard onto the floor and stormed out as quickly as they had stormed in. Amburo's mother, with a broken mind, body, and spirit, was barely able to crawl to her son, praying for him to be alive, not knowing if they killed him. It took all the strength she could muster to untie the boy and cradle his barely alive body in his arms. Tears were blurring her vision as she wailed, holding her son's limp body.

This night terror would jolt Amburo awake, bolting him upright, in a cold sweat, gasping for air. There were other triggers that would cause Amburo to have flashbacks. Sometimes, a person walking by flicking their lighter as they lit a cigarette, would trigger a flashback. With a simple flicking of the lighter, he would immediately envision the time he and his mother were forced to watch the soldiers burn his childhood home. The soldiers ripped Amburo's stuffed bear out of his arms and laughed as they threw the last thing Amburo's father ever gave him into the fire. His father had been murdered for trying to protect his wife and son from the infernal evil that tore their country apart. This is the flashback Amburo was visualizing as he stood there waiting for the girls to come out of baggage claim.

Chapter 8

A passenger from a recent flight was hailing a cab when he accidentally bumped into Amburo, snapping him out of his flashback. Amburo remembered to hold up his cardboard sign with the girls' names on it as the girls were exiting the baggage claim. They saw their names and immediately headed to the Town Car and settled inside while Amburo put their luggage in the trunk. After sleeping for the entire flight, the girls were well rested and ready to start partying again. Michele was quick to open the complimentary bottle of Champagne from the resort. It was such a quick jaunt from the airport to the hotel that the girls barely had enough time to finish their glasses of Champagne. Mateo Becerra, the bellhop for the resort, was quick to open the Town Car's door and greet Party and Michele with the well-scripted greeting he is required to give all guests. Mateo escorted the girls to the front desk and suggested they check in while he retrieved their bags. Mateo was what some people would call slow. He never finished school and had the equivalent of a third-grade education. It was his mother, who was head of housekeeping that got him the job as a bellhop. Mateo was an incredibly happy-go-lucky guy who was excellent with even the rudest of guests. It was his personality that made it difficult for anyone to be cruel to him. However, it was his cognitive challenges and his all-around good and trusting nature that made it easy for the wrong people to take advantage of him, especially a certain co-worker who said he was his friend. It was easy for that certain co-worker to get Mateo to do things he should not be doing. Easy as taking candy from a baby, you might say. He met the girls back at the front desk and escorted them to their room. Right away, Michele took a liking to Mateo, which was out of character for her. She always looked down at the wait staff and others who served the public. Not tipping or leaving a penny for a tip was a stunt she was known for. Every time Patty, Josh, and Michele went somewhere, either Josh or Patty would make an excuse to go back into the restaurant and hand the wait staff a five or ten-dollar bill and apologize for Michele's stunt. Not this time, though. Right away she got the feeling Mateo was a person she needed to be nice to, making sure she thanked him and gave him a good tip once they got to the room. As Mateo was leaving, he said to Michele he would have the bartender send up another bottle of Champagne. Once Mateo left, Patty went to the mini bar and checked out the selection while Michele wasted no time changing into her bikini. Michele looked over at Patty saying, "Forget the minibar. Get changed, we'll hit the poolside bar instead. I want to check out the guys." Patty loved that idea, thinking that this is the road to Michele breaking up with Josh, hoping saving herself for him would pay off. Patty heard a knock at the door while she was changing. She didn't pay too much attention, knowing Michele would answer the door.

Immediately after leaving Michele and Patty's room, Mateo went to the poolside bar where his co-worker, friend, and bartender, Jeremy Phillips was. As always, Mateo would tell Jeremy when either a single woman or a group of women arrived without male counterparts. He would tell Mateo he was specifically looking for blonde women, especially those, as he would say to Mateo, with nice tatas. Jeremy would always give Mateo a twenty-dollar bill and tell him he was his favorite co-worker and best friend at work. Being Jeremy's favorite and best friend alone would have been enough for Mateo. The twenty dollars he got every time only sweetened the deal for him. Mateo asked once why Jeremy wanted him to report the specific women to him. Jeremy had told Mateo there was a secret place he took those special guests to. He told Mateo that certain guests get to go to this secret place for "special treatment" that no other guest is allowed to have. Mateo tried to ask more about the secret place, only to have Jeremy interrupt by saying Mateo isn't supposed to know about it because the "special guests" want to keep it a secret. It was a very private club that no one else could know about, "VIPs only" he said. He told Mateo he could lose his job if anyone found out he told him about it. He also said to Mateo he wanted to keep a close eye on them to make sure they got exactly what they came to Mexico for. He reminded Mateo that best friends do not tell on best friends. If Mateo wanted to be best friends, he could not talk about it to anyone. He had to keep the secret. Nobody can find out. Mateo loved his best friend like a brother, so he was happy to keep it a secret. This time, as Mateo was headed to tell Jeremy about the "special guests" with the nice tatas, he had an uneasy feeling. The blonde was nice to him and gave him a twenty just like his best friend would do. As Mateo approached Jeremy, the uneasy feeling quickly became a gut-wrenching bad feeling. Mateo did not want to tell Jeremy about the guests he just left but if he didn't, Jeremy would get mad at him and not want to be best friends anymore. The thought of that upset Mateo a great deal. He did not want to lose his best friend. As he would always do, Mateo gave Jeremy the signal by telling him the guest's room number and that he needed a complimentary bottle of Champagne. Jeremy knew this was the signal because only "special guests" would receive a second complimentary bottle of Champagne. Jeremy would slip a twenty-dollar bill into the cocktail napkins he would place on the serving tray. Mateo would quickly deliver the Champagne to the room. After retrieving his reward hidden inside the cocktail napkins, he would knock and leave the tray outside the room, then rush back to his station to help the next guests with their bags and get them settled in.

Jeremy Philips was a young man in his late twenties. Jeremy worked hard to maintain the well-sculpted muscular body with the well-defined six-pack abs the women loved. At least that is what he told himself. The girls Jeremy was with really did not say anything because they could not. Jeremy was not blessed with facial symmetry, so what he lacks in symmetrical features he made up for with a well-toned body. His sculpted chest and lean body mass also make up for the lack of endowment with the other male muscle. Jeremy grew up in a small rundown, rat-infested, and dilapidated trailer park just outside of El Paso, Texas, close to the Mexican border with his foster mother. His foster mother, Patrica Jones, who everyone called Trixie, was the epitome of trailer trash. She was always dressed in tight leopard print mini dresses, which would reveal she was wearing her Tuesday panties on a Saturday night. Her blonde hair was always done up in a big hairdo, which required the use of the entire spray can of Aqua net. Some say the hairdo was so popular that it alone caused the hole in the ozone layer in the 1980's. Trixie was a waitress at the local dive bar. This roach infested hole in the wall bar was where the single women from the trailer park would go on a Saturday night, looking to get laid. The young Army recruits from Fort Bliss knew this. Cheap booze, loose women, and one-night stands were incentive enough to pack the place every Saturday night. It was argued that the building that looked like it was built out of used pallets and plywood sat one foot inside of Mexico. Thus, Texas's drinking age laws did not apply, and the local LEO's had no jurisdiction. The young recruits knew it was the easiest place to go wild and let loose. It was just far enough outside the city limits and just barely inside Mexico that the MP's did not bother with the place. This is also the bar where Jeremy was conceived. His birth mother lived in a trailer on the other side of the trailer park. She never married Jeremy's bio dad: never really knew who he was and never tried to find out. The only thing Priscilla Philips knew about the guy was that his military ID was fake. One night in the sack, and he was never to be seen again. Because of this, Jeremy was given his mother's last name. It was Trixie who helped with Priscilla's care when she was diagnosed with stage four terminal lung cancer when Jeremy was just three years old. Medicare and Welfare stepped in to help pay for her medical expenses and childcare. Trixie had been friends with her for years; they were like sisters. Since Priscilla had no family nor did she know who Jeremy's father was, they gave Trixie a caregiver's stipend. Trixie was quick to agree to become the legal guardian since they offered to pay her to be Jeremy's foster mother once Priscilla passed. Trixie never passed up free money from the state and free food stamps.

Trixie was never married and mostly lived alone in her 1968 single-wide trailer, which was one of the newer models in the park. Her on again off again, over-the-road truck driver boyfriend would stay with her from time to time between runs. Mack Harris was an independent trucker who owned his own rig and loved his job because he never wanted to be tied down. Being an over-the-road truck driver, he could be gone on a haul for weeks or even sometimes months. When he needed a break from the road, he would always show up at Trixie's place. Mack was your typical rural, beer-swilling, cigarette-smoking, uneducated redneck with a pack of Reds rolled up and tucked under the sleeve of his tee shirt, and a single cigarette tucked behind his ear. Hank was the type of guy who viewed women as personal property. His favorite saying was, "There are only two places a woman belongs: in the kitchen, and in the bedroom, and they best be good at both." Much to Trixie's surprise, Mack loved the idea of Jeremy living with her. He always wanted a son, but never the responsibility that went along with having a son. This was the perfect set up for him. He did not have to pay for Jeremy or raise him; that was all on Trixie. When Hank got tired of playing house and pretending to be a family, he would just go back out on the road till he was struck with the urge to come back. Mack wasted no time in mentoring Jeremy in his redneck ways. Hank was a huge influence on Jeremy's upbringing. First, by teaching then three-year-old Jeremy how to properly slap Trixie on the ass. Later, when Hank would rough Trixie up in front of Jeremy because his morning eggs were served scrambled instead of sunny side up or his coffee was not hot enough, it would cause the now six-year-old Jeremy to cry. Thinking he was being a good dad, Hank would take Jeremy for ice cream, just the guys. He would explain to Jeremy that this was the proper way to treat a woman, and he needed to learn this now if he was going to grow up right. "Hank doesn't raise no sissy boys." He would bellow all proud and full of himself. The unfortunate part was that Jeremy was a quick study. It was Jeremy's high school and teenage years that this behavior came out, both at home and with his girlfriends. Jeremy would always look for girls who had a single mom or an absentee dad. He liked it even more when the older brother was what he referred to as a "MEGA-nerd." Guys who were nerds were not known to get into fights, nor would they stand up to the guy taking full advantage of their sister. One night, Jeremy and a girl he was dating were alone on a Saturday night in Jeremy's bedroom. Both had just turned fourteen and were sitting on Jeremy's bed, kissing. Shelia Long was the type of girl he liked, was googly-eyed over him, with no father or brothers, and a welfare mother who was strung out more often than not. He got her to agree to him kissing and touching her breasts only. Of course, being a fourteen-year-old with raging hormones and not knowing how to control his primal urges, Jeremy didn't stop just feeling her breasts. He pushed her onto her back, got on top of her, forced himself between her legs, and started dry humping her. Although it felt good, Shelia wanted to stop and asked Jeremy to stop. Instead of stopping, he kept humping her and started to lick her nipples, which immediately caused them to become erect. The sensation caused Shelia to groan with pleasure. She arched her back into Jeremy's crotch. Although she was enjoying it, she still wanted him to stop. She was not ready to go all the way. Jeremy would not stop; he pushed himself up and knelt between Shelia's legs. He unzipped his pants and slid them down, exposing himself to her. Shelia could not help but laugh, confusing Jeremy. He demanded to know what she was laughing at. She pointed to his manhood and said through her laughter, "Oh, my gawd! It's so small!" That was the trigger that caused Jeremy to snap. With an open hand, he slapped Sheila upside her head, stunning her long enough for Jeremy to rip off her green neon miniskirt. She started to get her wits about her as he was ripping the matching tights and leg warmers off. Shiela started to scream, but Jeremy quickly covered her mouth with his hand. He leaned forward, overpowering her and began to force himself inside her. He was barely able to penetrate her as he raped her.

Shelia lay there terrified of him and what he was doing. She started swinging her arms wildly, slamming her fists onto his back trying to break free and get him to stop raping her. This turned Jeremy on even more. The more she resisted, the hotter it got for him, quickly bringing him to climax with screams of, "OH GOD! I AM CUMMING BABY! I'M CUMMING!" When he was done, Shelia lay on the bed crying. Jeremy demanded she stop. He said she asked for it, that's what you get for laughing at me. Shelia screamed at him. "FUCK YOU! You raped me, I am calling the cops!" as she tried to get away from him, Jeremy was too quick for her. He grabbed her and pinned her down again, shoving her own torn panties into her mouth to silence her. Just like Hank showed him, he began roughing her up and hitting her in places like the back of her head and other areas on her body where clothing would hide the bruises. When he was done roughing her up, she promised not to go to the police or tell anyone what happened. She was begging for her life. Begging so he would not follow through with his threat to kill her. She knew that he would kill her if she told anyone about the rape. Jeremy also told her she was now his girlfriend, making her his property, and she was to obey him or else. Shelia would endure this torture for the next four years. She had no one to turn to, no one to protect her. It was that or be beaten to death. Although suicide had crossed her mind many times in those four years, death was never really an option for her.

It was Jeremy's eighteenth birthday; the day Trixie would lose her free money. No more free money from the state meant Jeremy had to move out or start paying room and board if he wanted to continue living there. It also came with conditions. He has to stop putting his hands on her, slapping her ass, copping a cheap feel by squeezing a boob, and forget about her being his property. He is an adult now, and he must grow up and start respecting her. She suspected that he was abusing his girlfriend but did not want to go there. Neither kid was hers, and now that he was eighteen and she was losing her state support, she considered him no longer her problem. That evening, when she told Jeremy her demands, he just laughed at Trixie. When she told him he had to keep his hands to himself. He walked up to her and grabbed her by the arm, squeezing hard enough to leave a bruise. He slapped her on the ass with his other hand, then reached up and squeezed her boob like he always did. He said to her as he was unbuttoning his pants, "I ain't no little boy anymore sweet momma. Maybe it's time I show you how much of a man I am." With his pants now around his ankles and his manhood fully exposed, he forced Trixie to look at him. She stopped giving Jeremy a bath when he was four. Hank said he was big enough to take a bath alone. This was the first time in fourteen years she had seen him naked. She looked down and with a big shit eating grin said. "Honey, that thing is so small! What do you use for a jockstrap? A rubber band and a peanut shell?" This infuriated Jeremy, and he immediately became unhinged. One blow to the gut was all it took to drop Trixie to the floor. He kneeled over her, grabbed a handful of hair on each side of her head, and slammed the back of her head off the kitchen floor. Trixie let out a screech and tried to push him off her.

"TINY!" He shouted in her face, then slammed her head off the floor a second time. This time her eyes rolled back in their sockets, and her pupils were no longer visible, only the whites of her eyes He lifted her head to his face and shouted, "Peanut shell for a jockstrap!" then slammed her head for a third time off the kitchen floor. As they say, "third time's a charm." Trixie's breathing gave way to a gurgling sound. Jeremy knew that sound and knew it well. It was the same gurgling sound his mother made as she took her last breath. Priscilla Philips was lying in her bed, hugging her three-year-old son when she lost her battle with lung cancer. Even at just the tender age of three, the death rattle was a sound Jeremy would never forget, as it was the sound that haunted him every night as he slept. As Jeremy held Trixie's head in his hands and kneeled over her limp body, he remained eerily calm. The beating he just gave Trixie caused an erection that he needed to take care of. Shelia was still at work at the What-a-burger, so he knew he would have to take care of it himself. This was something he did not like doing, but he needed to get off in the worst way. He wondered if he got this fetish from his mother or the father he never knew. He decided to take care of his erection in the shower so he could get any evidence of Trixie off him at the same time.

Jeremy threw all his clothes into a duffle bag, gathered up a few things from his room, and loaded Trixie's car. He went into the kitchen. Being careful not to step in the pool of blood that was around Trixie's head, he headed for the coffee can on top of the refrigerator, knowing that was where Trixie's secret stash of cash was. He took the money and counted it. There were close to a thousand dollars in ten, twenty, fifty, and a few one-hundred-dollar bills. Taking the can, his duffle bag, and grabbing Trixie's car keys from her bedroom, he headed out to the carport. Sitting behind the wheel of Trixie's car, Jeremy knew he had at least a two-hour head start before Shelia would find Trixie's dead body. He knew he would be well over a hundred miles inside of Mexico before they would even start to look for him. Four days later, he arrived in the resort town of Cancun. Because gas and food were so cheap in Mexico, along with sleeping in the car, he barely put a dent in the wad of cash he had. Knowing he still had plenty of money, he decided to lie low in a remote town about fifty miles south of all the resorts in Cancun. When he felt enough time had passed and no one came looking for him, he got a job as a bartender in a couple of local taverns around Cancun. This is where he met Mateo, who, with the help of his mother, got him a job at the hotel.

Chapter 9

Michele had already finished changing into her bikini when there was a knock at the door. The knock was accompanied by a male voice saying, "Room service I am here with a complimentary bottle of the resort's finest Champagne." Michele wasted no time answering the door and allowed Jeremy to enter the room carrying a big silver tray with the Champagne on ice and two Champagne flutes. Jeremy made his way into the room. He had already unbuttoned the top three buttons of his white-collared shirt, showing off his freshly waxed chest. His well-defined upper torso with the perfect V-shape did its part to catch Michele's eye. With a big smile, he used his self-proclaimed award-winning personality, and introduced himself. "Hi, I am Jeremy." With a wink, he flashed an even bigger cheesy smile, trying to be sexy he said, "but you can call me anytime." The girls giggled at his attempt to flirt. "I do not do this for all the guests, but I will make an exception for lovely ladies. I will be your personal bartender and social director. I will take care of your every need, and I do mean every need." Patty blushed when he said, "every need." Michele cozied up to him laying a hand on his chest, seductively biting her lower lip then told him, "My name is Pandora, and I just might have a box for you to open." Jeremy was pleased that it was the blond girl with the big tatas who took the bait. Even though Patty was "doable" his fetish revolved around the ones who looked like his mother. Jeremy knew it was time to leave. The reason was not because he was still on duty at the poolside bar. He had to leave because seeing Michele's well-formed breasts with her nipples protruding through the fabric and the mention of the "box" she offered up, caused a stirring in his pants. Jeremy gently took the hand Michele had on his chest and softly kissed her hand. He looked into Michele's eyes and said, "I would love to stay longer but I need to get back." Letting go of her hand, he started to leave. When he got to the door, he turned back and told the girls he would have more Champagne waiting for them at the poolside bar, then walked out of the room gently closing the door behind him. Jeremy was feeling damn proud of himself as he casually strolled back to the poolside bar. Last time he used that pick-up line on a female "VIP" guest, her husband, who Mateo did not know was with her, walked in as he was saying, "You can call me anytime." Jeremy was caught off guard but was quick to add, "you need something from the bar." It came out so smooth and casually, both the husband and wife thanked him saying they would keep that in mind. This time no one interrupted him, and the hot blond chick with the big tatas offered up her box. Mateo did well.

Patty had never been to a resort like this and like her parents, except for the Woodstock festival back in sixty-nine, had never traveled outside of Maine. Michele on the other hand, had frequented resorts like this often with her parents during their school's winter breaks. Patty was brimming with excitement. She wanted to explore every inch of the resort. She was gobsmacked the moment they got out of the Town Car in front of the grand entrance to the resort. It was breathtaking, with its large fountain centered in the circular drive. The fountain featured three statues, one in the shape of a logger head turtle flanked on each side by dolphins all spewing water into the air. The water was falling back into the blue tiled pool that surrounded the three statues. On each side of the large, glassed grand entrance was a garden filled with native flowering plants and several varieties of palms indigenous to the Gulf Coast of Mexico. Patty especially loved the floral pattern in the carpeted areas that had upholstered chairs and sofas for guests to use as a waiting area. The rest of the hotel lobby floor featured a unique granite only found in Italy. The Italian granite floors led from the grand entrance to the front desk and elevators. The lobby itself was colossal, with towering ceilings. It housed its own live garden large enough to hold a lofty palm tree and a fountain shooting water straight up towards the towering glass ceiling. The corridors and guest rooms were carpeted with a tropical floral pattern. The two-bedroom suite the girls had was exquisitely decorated in true five-star fashion. Michele told Patty the only exploring she wanted to do was by the pool bar. Patty chugged the last of the Champagne she was drinking. She told Michele that after hanging out at the pool, she wanted to take a sunset walk on the beach, The bubbly Champagne caused her to do a soul-leaving-your-body belch that came out as BRAAAAAEACHHH. Both girls laughed; the alcohol was starting to make them silly. When they finally got to the pool, a bottle of Champagne was waiting for them. Michele flirted with Jeremy while the girls enjoyed a few more glasses of Champagne. Patty decided to walk the beach the hotel fronted while Michele flirted with Jeremy.

Chapter 10

In the pitch black of night, under a cloudless sky with millions of stars shining brightly in the Everglades swamp, the young woman slept behind the wheel of her Fiero. The empty bottle of Tequila lay on the floor of the passenger side, and the vodka bottle was tucked back in her bag. It was not long before her eyelids started their nightly twitching. Behind the closed eyelids her eyes were rapidly moving, she was in the sleep stage known as REM sleep. The alcohol did nothing to stop the dream which would quickly turn into another one of her nightmares. The young woman had been having nightmares for the past few months. They would always start as a pleasant dream then quickly turn into a horrifying nightmare. When she woke from the nightmare, she would bolt up in bed, in a terrified state of panic, gasping for air. The tee shirt and panties she wore to bed would be soaked from the cold sweat that had broken out. It would take several minutes to fully wake up and calm her breathing, and herself, back down. She always woke up thinking she was still in the nightmare. There was that one night, the nightmare she was having turned into a full-blown night terror causing a panic attack that would not quit. She had gotten a room at the Holiday Inn in Rocky Mount North Carolina. Normally she would sleep in her car at a truck stop or rest area that allowed overnight parking. There was never a shortage of those on Route 95. After a few grueling nights fending off the lot lizards who would knock at her car window asking if she was in need of a blow job not realizing it was a female that was sleeping in the car at the truck stops or old trolls who cruised the rest areas looking for a young male travelers in hopes of giving them oral pleasure, she needed a safe place and a real bed to sleep in. The Holiday Inn Travel Lodge was directly off the highway and had the best rate advertised on their flashing roadside sign. Just $29.99 free cable and color tv. *Who could pass that up.* She thought to herself as she pulled into the parking lot.

After settling into her room, and feasting on a true-blue, old fashioned, home-cooked southern dinner, (at least that's what the sign in the window said), from the diner at the end of the parking lot, and a long hot shower from the motel that advertised at the check in desk "long hot showers at no extra charge." She pulled the covers off the bed back, fluffed the pillows, turned on the free HBO, and wanted nothing more than to have a quiet and relaxing evening. She wanted to take her mind off the events that had been going on in her life. Checking the channel guide, she saw "The Texas Chainsaw Massacre" was coming up next. She thought to herself. *This is exactly what I need to relax.* She jumped into bed, not realizing just how exhausted she was, and fell right to sleep as the movie was starting. It was not long before the pleasant dream started. She always remembered what she dreamt about. The dreams always started off as warm and pleasant before the nightmare would take over. Tonight, the nightmare turned into a full-blown night terror so horrifying it would haunt her for the weeks to come. She started thrashing and screaming in her sleep. The thrashing was so violent she sent the lamp on the night table next to the bed crashing into the floor. The bed's headboard kept slamming against the wall, waking the older couple in the next room who called and notified the front desk, demanding they call the police. "Someone is being raped or murdered! NO! Someone is being murdered I am sure of it!" was what the older woman was screaming to her husband from across the room as he was telling the front desk what was going on. Within minutes the Rocky Mount Police were pounding on the door to the room the young woman was in. "This is the police is everything ok. Open the door for us." The young woman had already stopped screaming and had awoken from her nightmare just before the police arrived. She was sitting up violently trembling from the night terror that rattled her to her core and held in her mind. It was the pounding on the door that brought her back to reality. She took a few deep breaths trying to get her wits about her again and help her think, feeling for and not finding the lamp that was now broken on the floor. With only the light from the television she got up and turned on the overhead light. She peered through the peephole and saw it was the police. With a few deep and calming breaths, she cracked open the door, poked her head out and coyly said, "What's the problem officer?" The Officer told her they had received a report of a disturbance coming from this room and he asked to be let in. The young woman complied and let the officer in. She assured the officer she was alone when he asked if anyone else was in the room. The Officer searched the small closet and bathroom then checked under the bed to find no one. He asked what happened to the lamp and why it was broken on the floor. Again, asking if she had anyone in the room and asking if they had left before he had gotten there. She once again assured him no one was there. She told the officer his knock startled her, and she accidentally knocked the lamp over trying to turn it on. Searching the room with his eyes while listening to the explanation the young woman was giving, he noticed what was on the TV and asked her to turn the volume up. As luck would have it, Sally Hardesty was well into her screaming scenes. The young woman was quick to tell the Officer she did not realize just how loud the TV was till she heard the woman in the next room banging on the wall yelling the police are coming. She knew this was a lie, but it came out so convincingly that the officer decided to wrap it up and finally left. The rest of the night there were no dreams, just the restful sleep for which she was longing. The following morning, she decided to head east towards Kentucky, for no particular reason.

Tonight's dream was different than other dreams. Before falling asleep she could not shake the weird feeling she had about Evan. "What was it about him that gave her this feeling?" is what she kept asking herself. She could have sworn he had an aura glowing around him but passed that off as glare from the headlights and the tequila playing tricks with her eyes. She took a few hits off the roach that was in her ashtray and a few more swigs of tequila thinking this would help calm her mind. Instead, as sleep took over, the dream started. In tonight's dream, she saw a woman she had never met. The woman wore a white flowing gown that seemed to gently float in a nonexistent breeze. Her hair was held in place with a crown made of daisies, purple statice, and waxflower. The unknown woman was standing in a beautiful meadow with swaying grass as high as her waist. The woman kept saying "He will be with his father soon." Then faded away as the young woman started to stir in her sleep and eventually woke from her dream. It was just past midnight October 30th, 1988, and it was still several hours before sunrise. It was much warmer than normal for this time of year. Warm enough that she started the car and put the AC on. She turned the map light on and picked up her notepad again, looking down at the few words she began to write earlier just before Evan showed up. She picked up her pen and wrote.

Trauma lies dormant in all of us. Just lying there waiting for one of life's triggers to wake it up. Leaving scars that never heal. Terror also lies in wait with its never healing scars. Neither know death like we do. Yet death is the only way to silence them.

Her eyes filled with tears; she put the pen down and placed the pad on the passenger seat. She did not want risk her tears staining her note pad like the other times. She reached under her seat for the gun. She placed the barrel of the gun under her chin as her crying got louder. She sat in the driver's seat sobbing. The tears running down her face and clear snotty fluid leaking from her nose. Her mouth was laced with drool as she wailed. "OH GOD! WHY ME WHY!" The hammer was cocked into position waiting for her finger to gently squeeze the trigger so it could do its job and strike the bullet freeing it from its chamber, bringing the peace she desperately sought.

Chapter 11

Patty never traveled far from the tiny Central Maine town where she lived, other than the trip to Woodstock, which she had no memory of since she was only two at the time. Because of that, this made seeing the white sandy beach stretching for miles and miles in both directions, and with the Caribbean Sea extending so far out that the water met the sky on the horizon, the most spectacular view she had ever seen. The convergence of the Earth and sky formed a line as far as her eyes could see, just like the beach did. This was an awe-inspiring and breathtaking sight to see for Patty. Patty loved to swim. She preferred going to Long Pond in Rome or over to Doloff Pond in Mount Veron versus swimming in Gibson's pool. She couldn't wait for her freshman year at Mercy College to start so she could swim in Big Lake for the first time. Big Lake was the largest and most popular lake in Southern Maine: One of the few lakes where the water meets the sky. Certain parts of Moose Head Lake and Grand Lake Matagamon were the two other lakes with the same amazing views where the water meets the sky. Patty strolled casually across the beach and wandered towards the water. The girls were warned of rip currents by Mateo when he escorted them and their luggage to their room. Even though Patty was a strong swimmer, she heeded the warning and did not wade too far out in the warm waters of the Caribbean Sea. Although the water was relatively calm, she was mesmerized and lost in the moment by the small waves rushing in, then rushing back out. The buzz from the Champagne made her unaware of the stingray she was about to step on. Her right foot came down on the fish that was hidden in the sand, startling her enough that she let out a screech, catching the attention of Blake Davies, the lifeguard who was on duty and standing close by at the water's edge. Blake rushed over to Patty as she fell backwards into the water. "Here, let me help you up." he said as he extended his hand to her. A red-faced Patty took his hand and allowed him to help her back up. Blake was what you would call an all-round nice guy. Always sporting a big, friendly smile, he was someone who took immense pride in his physical appearance, including his no tan lines deep golden tan. When Blake was not on the beach working his lifeguard job, you could find him in the resort fitness gym or nude sunbathing in the private courtyard of his small house on the outskirts of town. Now, back on her feet, Patty said to Blake. "This may sound stupid, but I think I stepped on a fish." Blake smiled as he told her it was not stupid and that she did step on a fish. He said it was a stingray. He could tell she had not been stung since she was not complaining about any foot pain. However, he still told Patty he should take her to his stand and check to make sure she had not been stung by the fish. Patty sat in the doorway of the tiny lifeguard hut with her leg up being supported by Blake who was down on one knee, "checking out" the bottom of Patty's foot. Patty was flirting away, playing the damsel in distress role with Blake. "Oh, does it look bad? If it weren't for you, I could have drowned or been swept away in a rip tide." Even though Blake was doing his best not to laugh, he could not hide his huge smile, which was a turn on for Patty. Blake did a little of his own flirting back. "It looks pretty bad; I think you may need to keep your foot elevated for at least a week. Who knows maybe more." His flirting came across as more serious than intended; the look on Patty's face showed she was taking him seriously. Blake saw this and told Patty he may know a way to prevent that. Patty asked what it was. Blake said. "There is this quaint little cantina in town that serves the best margaritas in all of Mexico. I heard that Margaritas are good for you after stepping on stingrays. Their Cochinita Pibil will melt in your mouth. Then maybe after, we can go dancing at the nightclub." Patty started laughing; she was not expecting to be asked out. There was no way she was going to say no to a date with Blake. She was quick to say, "Yes, but on one condition." Blake smiled as he asked what the condition was. Patty leaned forward as Blake gently released her foot, tilted her head slightly, and said," You have to kiss me." Blake was eager to oblige. She slid her tongue into his mouth, running it across his teeth. His teeth were as perfectly smooth as they were perfectly white when he flashed his big smile. Blake was quick to return the favor with his tongue exploring Patty's mouth while gently caressing her inner thighs with his hands. They both pulled back at the same time and Blake slid his hand towards her knees and eventually removed them from her legs. "How about I pick you up around eight tomorrow night?" "Perfect" she said as she leaned in and started kissing him again.

After Patty left to walk the beach, Michele moved her seat and sat at the far end of the bar away from everyone so she could flirt with Jeremy. The pool area and the hotel was sparse as far as guests go. June is part of the off-season. This gave Jeremy some extra time to talk to Michele. Michele was seated in the one section of the bar that was out of view from both the pool and Jeremy's supervisors. The resort was one of the only resorts that was locally owned, unlike the other resorts which were owned by the large hotel chains. This resort was owned by the Diaz family, one of Mexico's infamous cartel families. The resort was their only legitimate business venture. The large amount of tax revenue they paid to the Servicio de Administración Tributaria, which is Mexico's version of the IRS, was used as bribe money. The Diaz's paid the local Federales extra tax money to look the other way when it came to the other family business. This was great for Jeremy, knowing he was most likely a wanted man for the murder of his foster mother Patrica Jones. He was able to work here and fly under the radar and not have his name run through US-based corporations where he may be flagged. Because of this, Jeremy worked hard to keep his bosses happy. There were also his special VIP guests, who the other resorts would catch onto very easily. This was a job he did not want to lose. While he was flirting with Michele, he made sure the supervisors saw him cleaning and stocking the bar too. Neglecting the bar was not tolerated; the Diaz family made sure they always kept up appearances. Jeremy had just finished his wipe down of the bar and made sure the few guests by the pool had full drinks before he went to talk with Michele. The flirting had gotten more serious and fun. Jeremy came back over, slid his hand between Michele's legs and gently massaged her thighs. This time, he slid his hand up and started to rub her private parts through her bikini. Michele let out a slight moan of pleasure. Jeremy continued to flirt with her while she enjoyed both the verbal and physical attention. Jeremy slightly shifted his hand as he tried to slide a finger under her bikini bottom and insert his finger into the warm and moist area between her legs. Even though Michele wanted him to do that to her right there, she teased Jeremy by gently pushing his hand away, saying, "That is going to cost you dinner and drinks first." If Jeremy had been back in Texas, he would have considered this a rejection. Which was something he never handled well and it led to him resorting to violence so he could get what he wanted. Here at the resort, it was part of his plan, she said exactly what he wanted her to say. Dinner and drinks were a perfect way to get his VIP guests off the resort's property. He flashed his lady-killer of a smile and asked Michele if tomorrow night they could have dinner at Navios Bistro, then drinks at the local disco-tech. Michele cordially accepted and let Jeremy go back to rubbing the outside of her lady parts till it was time for Jeremy to make his pool rounds. Before she left to go back to her room, she let Jeremy do to her what he was trying to do earlier to, as they say, "to seal the deal.

Chapter 12

After an uneventful evening of room service and falling asleep from a full belly of hotel food, several glasses of Champagne, and being exhausted from traveling, the girls woke up early the next morning full of excitement. The suite Michele's father booked had a living room as you entered. On each side of the living room were the entrances to the bedrooms. Patty and Michele each had their own private bedroom. Patty was sitting up in bed hugging her knees thinking about Blake. She was reconsidering giving up her virginity versus saving herself for Josh. She thought to herself, *what the hell. It's not like he is a virgin either.* Although she was thinking that way, there was a part of her that could not help but feel a little guilty if she did let Blake take her virginity. Just as she decided it would be OK, she wouldn't tell Josh, she felt a warm and moist feeling in her panties. Patty knew right away what was happening and the horrible timing it was. It took her by surprise because the cramping she always got did not happen, and she was at the very least a week early or so she thought. The decision of whether or not to sleep with Blake was now made for her. She got up, grabbed a Tampax out of her suitcase, and headed to the bathroom to take care of business and shower.

Michele was up, showered, and ordered room service for them while Patty was still in her room. She was deciding on what she wanted to do for the day. Did she want to hang out by the pool and do more teasing with Jeremy or hang out on the beach and check out who she wanted to hook up with next? Room service had just left the breakfast cart when Patty emerged from her bedroom. The girls decided to have their breakfast on the balcony overlooking the beach. Michele rolled the room service cart out to the balcony; Patty grabbed some brochures of the local attractions to look over while they both ate. Michele started to tell Patty about her flirting with Jeremy. She told Patty about letting Jeremy fondle and rub her through her bikini bottom. She revealed her intended plan for their time there, which was to have a different guy or guys in her bed every night. Michele even told Patty not to be afraid to join in if she wanted. Patty was getting annoyed with Michele's flirting; she was Josh's girlfriend after all. She had no intention of joining in on the sexcapades nor did she want anyone but Josh inside her. Patty only went on the pill because she felt pressured by Michele to do it together. Patty did not let her annoyance show, though. In the back of her mind this was going to be the trip that finally would get Michele to dump Josh, and she would be right there to give Josh a shoulder to cry on and then finally lose her virginity to the love of her life. Patty did not acknowledge the invitation to join in. She also did not tell Michele her cycle just started, so there was going to be no one in her this week. She did tell Michele about Blake, the dinner date and Disco they were going to. Michele finally noticed the brochures that Patty laid on the table and picked the one for Captain Jack's snorkeling adventure. On the cover was a picture of Captain Jack in his Navy uniform with the caption, "Meet your snorkeling adventure host, retired Navy Captain Jack O'Malley." Michele looked at the picture thinking it must be an old picture because this guy looked too young to be a Captain or retired. She said to Patty, "Hey, this looks like it would be totally rad! Let's do it!" Patty did not hesitate to say, "That looks bitchin! I'm in for sure." The girls decided this is how they were going to spend the day.

When they arrived at the marina they quickly went over to where Captain Jack was docked. The first thing that went through Michele's mind was *HOLY SHIT! The picture wasn't old he really is that hot in person.* She was not into older guys, but Jack looked like he was in his twenties. She had to know, so after the brief introductions, the flirting began with her asking how someone so young could be retired. Patty rolled her eyes because she knew what Michele was up to and figured she would be snorkeling alone because Michele would be trying to get in this guy's pants. Jack smiled and said he joined the Navy right out of high school. He rose in ranks quickly because of his willingness to do repeated tours during the Vietnam War. His thirty-eighth birthday marked twenty years in the Navy, so he retired and followed his dream of owning a tour boat in Mexico. He told the girls, since it is off season, they would have the boat to themselves today. He wasted no time going over the safety rules and snorkeling instructions. After he finished with that, he untied the boat and headed out to the reef. Jack dropped anchor and told the girls this was the best spot; it was where all types of turtles gathered. Patty was eager to get into the water, so she immediately geared up and jumped in. She was pleasantly surprised when Michele jumped in right behind her. Patty could not hide the surprised look, and Michele knew why she got the look. She smiled at Patty and said, "I've got to do something in between the sex. Plus, Josh is going to want to hear about the trip I've got to have something to tell him." Patty just blew off what Michele said, dropped the mask over her eyes, and told Michele, let's get to it. She put the snorkel's mouthpiece in and started exploring the marine life below. As they swam around on the surface, they were astonished by the beauty of the reef. They swam open-eyed, gawking at the undersea world that, until now, had only existed in the marine biology class from junior high school. Seeing this marine wonderland in person was awe inspiring for them. The reef displayed its majestic colors for the girls as if it were alive and knew it had to put on a show for them. There were pieces of coral so rich in color it was like staring at an underwater rainbow. The deepness of the purples in the blue crust coral and reds of the gorgonian coral were perfectly accented by the bright yellows and oranges of the cup corals. As they further explored, they came across sea whip coral teaming with schools of fish, so brilliant with color they were almost neon in appearance. The Rock Beauty Angelfish was displaying its stunning colors, from a bright yellow head and gills to its dark purple body. This was something only seen in their textbooks. The Blue Tang's color was a shade of blue the girls had never seen before and could only be found in nature. It was Michele who spotted the different turtles swimming around. Patty, who read the informational leaflet the captain handed out, was quick to identify the turtle as a Hawksbill turtle. The girls floated just at the surface of the water, watching a Loggerhead turtle swim beneath them. Patty and Michele had discovered a magical world they never wanted to leave. There was a feeling of peace and solace in the world they just discovered and never knew existed.

Captain Jack sounded the air horn to summon the girls back to the boat. Normally, the tours lasted two hours during the busy season, but Captain Jack gave the girls an extra hour since there was nothing else booked. The slow season was a suitable time to give tourists some extra time in the reef. Michele and Patty could not believe just how fast the time went. Both wanted to stay longer. As the girls climbed back aboard the boat, cocktails were waiting for them, just as the brochure promised: Captain Jack's very own frozen margaritas, along with some shrimp he'd barbecued while the girls were snorkeling. Once they were back on board, Michele wasted no time flirting with Captain Jack again. Patty did not want to be a witness to this. With a frozen margarita in hand and a belly full of shrimp, she headed to the bow of the boat with the excuse of wanting to sunbathe. Jack offered to show Michele the bridge of his boat. Michele looked puzzled; she had no clue as to what the bridge of a boat was. Captain Jack noticed her confusion and explained with a smile, "It's an old Navy term. It's where the captain of the boat sits and performs his duties." Michele tilted her head down, biting her lower lip, and gave Jack a seductive smile, as if to say "yes". Jack led the way up the narrow and steep steps to the bridge which was an enclosed room with a large Captain's chair in front of an instrument panel that looked out over the endless blue of the Caribbean Sea. Michele stood to Jack's left side just slightly behind him as he took a seat in his chair and showed her the instrument panel. Without Jack noticing, Michele had slid her bikini bottom off, then reached over and started rubbing Jack's crotch as she came around to the front of him and straddled his lap. Jack gently caressed Michele's back as he slid his hand up to untie her bikini top and tossed it to the floor. Seeing her more than bountiful breasts was all that was needed for little Jack to rise to the occasion. Jack leaned forward and started licking and gently teasing her nipples with his tongue. Michele unbuttoned and unzipped Jack's acid washed denim shorts releasing what was inside them. Whispering in Jack's ear she said, "Permission to put the torpedo in the tube Captain?" Jack smiled at the Navy reference and granted permission. Jack kept licking, nibbling, and fondling her breasts. Michele threw her head back and rode him as hard as she could. Things kept heating up and getting more intense. Jack leaned forward, and with Michele's legs wrapped tightly around him, stood up and stepped behind his chair, where he had room to lay Michele down on the floor, so he could thrust himself in and out of her with more force. It was not long before Michele's back arched up and she started gasping breathlessly, saying she was going to cum. Jack was there too. He looked down at her and said, "I am ready to release the torpedo. OH GOD fire in the hole," as his tense body started to ejaculate inside her. Michele had already begun to climax, and she was squeezing Jack as hard as she could, intensifying the sensation. When they were done Jack rolled off Michele and they lay next to one another catching their breath. Jack started laughing and telling Michele that this was the first time he used Navy slang for sex.

About an hour later, they were back at the pier with the boat docked and secured. The girls gathered their belongings and headed back to the hotel for a much-needed shower before their dinner dates. Jack was doing his normal end-of-day routine of cleaning the grill and restocking the mini bar when Amburo jumped off the dock and onto the boat. Jack turned to Amburo asking him, "How many times do I have to tell you, you need to ask permission before boarding a vessel?" Amburo laughed, and in a deep, heavy, African accent said, "That fake navy shit doesn't work on me. I know you came to Mexico to dodge the draft." Yeah, well, the retired Vietnam Vet and Navy bit gets me customers, plus what happened in the Sixties stays in the sixties." Not only did Jack lie about his age and his military service, but he also lied about why he was living in Mexico. Jack's number was picked in the first draft lottery of the Vietnam War, and his draft notice came in December of 1969, six months before his twenty-sixth birthday. He was adamant about protesting the war. There was no way he was going to fight in a war that he was so against; he was going to burn his draft notice and dodge the draft. Canada and Amsterdam were the most common destinations for draft dodgers. Jack figured Mexico would be the place that no one would look for him, and he was right. He snuck into Mexico shortly after his name was drawn on December 1st, 1969. It was January of 1970 that he first discovered Cancun and decided to hide out there in a little beach shanty hidden in the sand dunes of the Playa Delfines section of Cancun. When the war finally ended, and President Carter pardoned the draft dodgers, is when he came out of hiding. Too embarrassed to return home to his family which had many members who served in both WWII and the Korean War, he chose to stay in Cancun and start his business. Amburo just shook his head at Captain Jack's reply while asking how today went. Jack told him to tell the boss all went as expected. The blonde is perfect for his plans. We've just got to get her away from the other one. Amburo nodded his head to acknowledge, saying, "Leave that up to me," because he knew exactly what to do.

Chapter 13

Patty was sitting on the balcony of their suite staring off into the distance thinking about Josh. She could not help but feel bad for him. Patty had passed out in the car when they were out bar hopping with Michele's cousin, having no clue as to what was going on in the van or even what Michele did with her cousin in the bedroom. She was, however, aware of what went on inside the bridge of the boat with Captain Jack. They were not exactly quiet about it, and it was a relatively small boat. She wanted to rip into her about screwing around on Josh. As much as she wanted to tell her to stop cheating on Josh, she decided not to for two reasons. One of those reasons was it was Michele's father who paid for the trip. The last thing she wanted to do was to ruin the trip or end her friendship with Michele. The second reason was that she was in love with Josh and was afraid to tell Michele how she felt about him. Patty was afraid it would ruin the friendship trio they had. Although Michele did not tell Patty she could join in with her and Josh, she had a feeling that Michele would want to be intimate with her. Being intimate with Michele was not what Patty wanted; it was about sharing Josh. The menage a trios was not her thing, even though she had thought about doing one with Michele and Josh. Patty was so deep in thought that she had not heard Michele calling her from inside the suite. It was when Michele had stepped out onto the balcony that Patty realized Michele was trying to get her attention. Michele was being her sarcastic self as she walked out onto the balcony. "Earth to Patty come in Patty, this is mission control." Patty smirked, "Sorry, was just vegging out." She loved Michele's sarcasm even if it was being directed at her. Michele told Patty that Blake was in the lobby waiting for her. Patty had lost track of time sitting there on the balcony, and even though she was ready for her date, she still hurried and double-checked her look in the mirror, making sure she had everything in her purse she needed. As she hurried out the door, she heard Michele say. "I hope you get laid tonight." She quickly replied, "Back at ya." She shut the door and headed to the lobby. Michele rolled her eyes at Patty, thinking to herself. *She is going to die a virgin.*

Blake was standing in the lobby as Patty came rushing down the corridor into the lobby. At first glimpse, she thought he looked just like Josh. He was dressed in the same Miami Vice suit that Josh always wore and was sporting his own version of a mullet haircut, which made him the spitting image of Josh. As Patty approached Blake, she said. "What a hottie! Looking all glam." Blake smiled and blushed a little; he always blushed when a girl found him hot. Surprisingly, he had not been on many dates before. There were a few here and there, but most of the girls he met were with their families on vacation. Not that he was trying to get in their pants, it was hard to get them away from their family. Some were there with their boyfriends, others on their honeymoon. Meeting someone like Patty was a rarity for Blake. Blake always remained a gentleman and never forced himself on a girl, but he was not a virgin either. One look at Patty in her red leather miniskirt and matching blouse made him at least want to try getting somewhere with her tonight. As the two greeted one another, Amburo was by the entrance, standing so one of the mammoth potted ferns kept him out of view. Seeing Patty with Blake was a great concern for Amburo, and he did not like seeing them together. He watched as Blake took Patty by the hand and headed out to the car that was waiting for them. Amburo took a step back, trying to stay concealed from view as they walked past. There was a white limo waiting for them in the circular drive with the driver standing by the open passenger door. Patty got in first, and as Blake was getting in, he stopped, turned his head, and looked back to the hotel entrance where Amburo was. There was no one there, but he did notice the large ferns were moving as if someone had brushed up against them.

Amburo pulled up to the hotel entrance in a rented Town Car just as Michele was walking out. Amburo had called her room just as Patty and Blake had driven off. He told Michele he would be picking her up and taking her to meet Jeremy. Because hotel employees were not allowed to fraternize with guests, Jeremy would be meeting her at the restaurant, and he would be using a rental car to take her there. Michele went right to the car and got in before Amburo could get out and open the door for her. They quickly dashed off to the restaurant where Jeremy was waiting. On the ride over, Michele was curious as to why she was getting a limo ride. Not that she minded being picked up in a limo, but she was still curious. Amburo did not have to come up with a cover story. The truth was, he worked at the hotel as a driver full-time and drove evenings for the Cartel family who owned the hotel. He did not do this for the money. He took the part-time job so he could keep tabs on the family for Jeremy. However, he did leave out the part about who owned the limo and did not really answer who he worked for in the evenings. He told her he owed Jeremy a favor, so he offered to give her a ride, since he needed to go in this direction anyway. When they reached the restaurant, Amburo escorted Michele into the restaurant's host station. The host told Michele their table was ready and escorted her to her seat. He handed her a drink menu and told her Jeremy would be arriving momentarily. Amburo went outside to the spot where Jeremy would be waiting for him after he dropped off the "Special VIP Guests." Amburo would let him know when he dropped off the VIP. He met Jeremy as always and was quick to let him know that Blake had taken the brunette out on a date. Unlike Amburo, Jeremy welcomed this news because it made it easier for him to separate the girls. Amburo also updated him on what Captain Jack told him earlier. Jeremy instructed him to meet him later at the Disco and headed inside to meet Michele.

Blake and Patty were seated in a small off-the-beaten-path bistro known for its authentic home-cooked meals. Their slogan was "Just like

Abuelita's." The bistro was quaint with the warm and cozy feeling of home. The host, who was also the owner, seated them and bragged about how all the decorations in the bistro were handmade and passed down through several generations, much like the recipes they cook with. This was one of Blake's favorite spots because he did not like tourist traps, nor was he comfortable in big crowds. Blake looked over at Patty as she sat quietly for a few moments. Patty was taking in the ambience of her surroundings. She could see why Blake loved this place, and she fell in love with it the moment she walked through the door. When Jeremy was in their room delivering the Champagne, she got a very uneasy feeling about him. His presence felt threatening to her, and she didn't feel safe around him. She did not say anything to Michele because, as always, Michele would have said it was all in her head. Not only that, Michele was also going to do what Michele wanted, regardless of what objection anyone had. Blake, on the other hand, was completely different. Patty felt at ease with Blake. She called it her woman's intuition when it came to certain people. Her intuition told her Jeremy was bad to be around, and Blake was safe to be around. Dressing like Josh and sporting a mullet like Josh helped her be comfortable around him. Deep inside she knew mother nature, making the decision about losing her virginity to him, played a role as well. If it were not for Josh, she could easily fall for Blake. Even though Blake knew Patty was going to be returning to her life and leaving him behind, Blake was falling in love with Patty. Patty noticed Blake looking at her, and it made her feel warm. He finally broke the brief silence with, "Which do you prefer, wine or a cocktail before dinner?" Even the wait staff could see the feelings they were developing for one another as they made small talk over their wine and appetizers.

Jeremy was seated with Michele, telling her how amazing she looked while they were enjoying their cocktails. Michele scooted her chair closer to Jeremy, so they were sitting next to one another. Michele, being Michele, did not waste any time. She let Jeremy know how the evening was going to go by running her foot up and down Jeremy's leg. Jeremy in turn slid his hand under the table and onto Michele's inner thigh and leaned closer so he could whisper in her ear. They were in a very dimly lit restaurant, famous for its romantic and discreet seating. The booths and tables were spaced far enough apart that intimate conversations were not overheard. The lighting was dim to help enhance the atmosphere. The wall coloring was a dark, almost blackish-brown tone. The wall hangings were made from rustic wood frames encasing red velvet sculptured wallpaper as though they were pieces of art. On various pedestals were statues of Eros, Cupid, and Venus, along with other goddesses of love from mythology. The restaurant is promoted as *Cancun's prominent five-star dining experience for romantic dinners*. Jeremy leaned further in towards Michele, resting his arm on the back of her chair, and with his hand, gently massaged Michele's shoulder. His other hand had made its way up her thigh far enough so that he knew Michele was not wearing any panties. She let Jeremy explore a little more before saying, "The three D's first." "The three D's?" he asked. "You know, Dinner, Drinks, and Dancing first."

He smiled, sliding his finger into her, as he leaned in and kissed her. She was all his and he knew it.

Outside the small Bistro, Patty suggested they skip the limo and walk to where Blake was going to take her, which was the Disco. The nice thing about the resort community and the area in general was you could walk to just about everything. She held Blake's hand and rested her head on his shoulder as they strolled down the street toward their destination. Patty felt safe with Blake, not because he was the type of guy a woman could feel safe with, not because he was the type of guy who knew "no" meant "no", and not because he treated people, in general, with respect. It was also not because he was exceptionally respectful to women and was someone they could trust. He was all that and more. The reason Patty felt the way she did had to do with the fact that in her mind everything about Blake reminded her of Josh. Patty was so desperately in love with Josh that tonight she envisioned herself walking down the street with Josh instead of Blake. The way Michele was acting on this trip and even the way Michele had treated Josh beforehand only added a deeper emotional attachment to her feelings for Josh. She was truly in love with Josh and wanted to be his wife and the mother of his children. She snapped out of her daze when Blake let go of her hand and slid his hand around her waist gently guiding her in front of him with his other hand holding the door open for her as they entered the disco tech. The 70's style discos were well on their way into obscurity and close to extinction in the states except for those die-hard holdouts. However, they were alive and well in Mexico and still tremendously popular in the Mexican resort communities. Resort goers liked revisiting the fond memories of life before marriage, kids, and careers that took over their carefree lifestyle. It was a carefree time in their life with the disco's playing a role in that carefree time, consequently giving them their popularity and continued success in Mexico. When they entered the Disco, the scene was straight out of 1977 right down to the retro carpeting in the lounge area that encircled the lighted dance floor, and a DJ booth looking down on the dance floor. Michele saw Patty and Blake enter the Disco. Michele waved and motioned for them to join her and Jeremy, who had arrived shortly before they had. Jeremy did not like the idea of Patty and Blake joining them, although he hid his dissatisfaction well. Intros were made and although Jeremy worked at the resort and Blake's lifeguard station was close to the resort's beach entrance, Jeremy had never met, nor did he even know who Blake was. Blake knew some of the staff at the resort like Mateo and his mother and the few who worked out in the resort's gym. However, Jeremy was a face he had seen before but never truly met nor were they ever introduced. After pleasantries were exchanged, Jeremy said, "Not to be rude but this is a Disco, so let's dance!" He took Michele by the hand and headed to the dance floor. Blake and Patty took a few quick swigs of their drinks, then joined them on the dance floor. The DJ was playing Gloria Gaynor's "I Will Survive", and Michele got lost in the beat and rhythm of one of her favorite dance songs. When the song ended, the DJ announced it was that time and the crowd made a circle around the dance floor as the DJ cued up and started playing The Bee Gee's, "Stayin Alive". The song was Jeremy's cue to enter the open dance floor doing his legendry impersonation of John Travolta's character Tony Manero. Jeremy frequented the Disco often enough that the crowd knew what to expect when the DJ cued up that song. Jeremy more than impressively lived up to that expectation. His dance moves were spot on to Travolta's and he even threw in a few of his own custom moves that the crowd loved. When the song finished, Jeremy went over to a bedazzled Michele and took her by the hand back out to the dance floor so they could slow dance to another Bee Gee's hit, "More Than a Woman". Patty and Blake were on the other side away from Michele slow dancing to the song with Blake's arms wrapped around Patty's lower back and her head resting on his chest as they swayed to the music. Once again, Patty was lost in the illusion of Blake being Josh. As the night started to wear on, Jeremy started to get frustrated with having Patty and Blake around. He wanted them to leave so he could move forward with his plans for his VIP guest. His frustrations were quickly eased when Patty and Blake finished their drinks and started heading for the door hand in hand. Michele saw this and thought maybe she would not die a virgin after all.

A short time later, Patty and Blake were walking hand in hand down the beach with their shoes off and enjoying the feeling of the sand between their toes. They finally stopped by the lifeguard shack that is stationed close to the pool entrance of the resort. As they stood there, wrapped in one another's arms under the light of the waxing moon, Patty reached up to caress the back of Blakes head and slowly guide his lips to hers. Locked deep in the passion of that kiss drove Patty back into her delusion about being with Josh. As deep into the delusion as she was there was that tiny little piece of consciousness that knew this was not Josh and glad that she had miscounted her twenty-eight-day cycle. Regardless of what was going on in her head it was what had started going on in Blakes pants that had caught her attention. She thought to herself *how am I going to tell him that Mother Nature was not allowing her to lose her virginity tonight.* Out of the clear blue sky, she remembered what Michele had said to her, "I get you are waiting for the right guy. But in the meantime, if you want to keep a boyfriend and not lose your virginity you need to at least use your hand or mouth." Giggling to herself and thinking *God Michele you are such a slut,* she took Blake by the hand and started heading for the resort. Blake resisted a little, saying, "Give me a minute I ahhh..." Patty smiled and said just hold your coat in front of it and pulled him along. They were in Patty's bedroom when they started kissing again, and it did not take but their lips meeting before Blake's pants showed Patty he was enjoying it and wanted more. They were kissing passionately while Patty unbuttoned Blake's shirt and slid it off, exposing his well sculptured chest and abs. She then reached down and cupped his bulging crotch as he slid her leather mini shirt and blouse off. As Blake was undoing the clasp to her bra Patty had unzipped his fly and reached in, caressing him through his BVDs. Blake dropped Patty's bra to the floor and reached down to her panties. Patty gently stopped him, saying, "I have a better idea." She undid the clasp on his pants and slid them down. She got on her knees and started caressing him with her mouth through his briefs causing Blake to groan with pleasure in response to her warm breath on him. Patty did not have to explain to him why she didn't want him to take her panties off, he figured that out on his own. He wanted to return the favor and pleasure her but understood why he could not and was content with letting Patty have her way with him this way. Patty had finished taking Blake's clothes off, he was lying on his back with his head propped up on the pillows as Patty crawled between his legs, spreading them, so he was fully exposed to her. Patty had never performed this on a guy before, and the thought alone got her going. Shutting her eyes, she lowered her mouth on Blake letting the passion take over. She gently took him deeper into her mouth testing the limits of her gag reflexes, finding she did not have any. This pleased her greatly, but it was the thought of Blake being Josh that drove her wild as she took him all the way into her mouth. His musky scent was like an aphrodisiac, causing her to surrender herself to her primal instincts, giving way to a powerful expression of sexual desire that she had never experienced before, and she never wanted it to end. Blake reached down and put a hand on Patty's head as he raised his hips, sliding himself deeper into her mouth, then lowering his hips, repeating the pattern of pleasure. Patty started bobbing her head up and down with the motion of Blake's hips. Patty eagerly took Blake's deep thrust into her mouth, matching his thrusts with her head. She took her free hand and started to fondle his swollen jewels. The feeling of her mouth, along with the gentle touching of his family jewels caused his eyes to roll back in his head and let out another moan of intense pleasure. He could not hold back any longer; he knew he was going to explode at any moment. He told Patty he was not going to last, expecting her to finish by hand. Hearing that, Patty started going even faster not letting him go. She started sliding her fingers further down hitting the sensitive spot behind his scrotum, causing Blake to lose control and start ejaculating like a volcano spewing lava. She kept going until he had no more to give causing her own orgasm. When it was over, Patty leaned forward kissing Blake's chest, cuddling close and holding him tight as they both drifted off to sleep.

Chapter 14

Sitting alone in the darkness of the Everglades with only the faint sounds of the swamp creatures in the distance, the young, weary traveler cried out, "WHY ME! OH GOD WHY ME!" one last time before pulling the trigger of the gun that she had pressed tightly to her right temple. She pulled the trigger, expecting her nightmare to come to an abrupt end with her bloody gray matter splattering the driver's door and window, leaving the gory stains that would eventually ooze to the floor mats like in a horror movie. "NO!" she screamed, pulling the trigger again and again. The gun just clicked. She kept screaming, "I JUST WANNA DIE! FOR FUCK'S SAKE JUST WORK!" With the gun still against her right temple, she slammed her left hand on the steering wheel; there was spit spewing from her mouth with every heaving breath from her chest. She realized the gun she bought from the unbathed, inbred asshole, as she would come to describe him, was jammed and misfiring. With her forehead now resting on the top of the steering wheel and the gun still pressed against her right temple, she tried one last time, begging for the gun to work, begging for an ending to the mental torture that she could not outrun. Once again, the gun just clicked. This time, the trigger locked itself in place so it could not be pulled again. The gun's trigger had jammed to the point that the gun was now completely useless. Completely exhausted, she let the gun fall from her hand and sat with her head hanging down, wailing out loud till her voice went hoarse and her throat dried. Completely spent, with tears running down her face, she sat silently till the sun rose on All Hallow's Eve. The woman dressed in white, and glowing, faded into the sawgrass. In the distance, you could see the red glowing eyes of Big Al sink down into the murky waters of the swamp. On the access road next to Big Al, the headlights of the Chevy K10 pickup truck went dark.

Chapter 15

Michele excused herself and headed to the ladies' room while waiting for the next round of fresh drinks that Jeremy had just ordered, to arrive at their table. Michele had not returned to the table when the cocktail waitress arrived with the drinks. After the cocktail waitress had set the drinks down and collected her tip, she rushed off to the next table, allowing the little pill that Jeremy slipped into Michele's drink to go unnoticed.

Michele was looking at herself in the mirror after running a brush through her hair and adjusting her makeup. She had had enough of the Disco; it was time to leave so she could be alone with Jeremy. After giving herself a good look, she removed her bra and unbuttoned a few more buttons on her blouse, exposing more cleavage. She gave herself one final look and thought the way her nipples showed through her white blouse was a nice touch. She knew Jeremy would get the message. Tucking her bra into her purse, heading for the door and back to the table, she had no idea what was to come later that night. She got back to the table, grabbed her drink, sat back down, and guzzled the watered-down Pina Colada. She could tell right away from the first sip of her first drink that the Disco was not using top-shelf rum, it had a watered-down taste. Leaning forward towards Jeremy, with her braless breasts dangling in front of him, he immediately got the message loud and clear. She started kissing him as he placed his hand on her thigh, gliding his fingers to that one spot men never seem to find. Without hesitation or needless feeling around, his fingers had found their target, sending sensations of intense orgasmic pleasure to the septal region of Michele's brain. Michele, in a low, moaning voice, said, "Let's find some place a little more private." Jeremy smiled as he told her he knew just the place. As she stood up from the table, she started feeling lightheaded and woozy. She thought to herself, *I guess they don't water down the drinks after all.* She grabbed the table with both hands to steady herself. After a moment, the woozy feeling left, and she had her balance back, if only for the moment. Amburo was out front with the back door to the Lincoln open and waiting for them. Things were starting to spin. Jeremy wrapped his arm around her to keep her from falling. He smiled at some of the people staring at them and said, "I guess they're not watering down the drinks anymore." To which most gave a smirk or light chuckle as they carried on with their business. Michele had lost consciousness just as she was being helped into the car by Jeremy. Before getting into the car, Jeremy confirmed with Amburo and asked if everything was all set. Amburo told him Captain Jack was already there and waiting for them. Jeremy nodded and said, "Take us to the hut so we can give her the VIP treatment." Joining the unconscious Michele in the back of the car, Jeremy smiled at the young woman like a hunter admiring his fresh kill.

Within minutes, they arrived at the one-room beach shanty well hidden in the sand dunes just a short distance from the Disco. The shanty's exterior was a well-weathered gray board and batten with several battens missing. The missing battens along with the aged, weathered boards, left cracks wide enough for someone to peak in to get a glimpse of the room. The tiny covered front porch had just two steps leading up to it. The front door was weather battered with rusted hinges and a clasp and padlock to keep unwanted guests out and the VIP's in. The lean-to-style roof barely provided enough headroom for the three men. The shiny new padlock sat on a shelf just inside the door. Jeremy would always replace the old lock after each of his "VIP Guests" visit was over. Captain Jack had arrived shortly before Jeremy and Amburo, letting himself in. Captain Jack opened the wooden shuttered, glassless, and screenless window with its rusty hinges that squeaked like a mouse when you opened it, to replace the stale air from that day's heat. The only window the shanty had was on the opposite side of the front door in the tiny ten-by-fifteen shanty. The only piece of furniture was an old metal bed frame, spotted with rust where the white-painted finish had flaked off. Closer to the mattress, on the lower part of both the head and footboard, were marks from the leather cuffs they used as bindings. As Jeremy carried Michele into the shanty, he could hear the loud crash of the surf and the rumble of thunder in the distance from the storm cell that was creating the rough surf. The beach was on the other side of the sand dunes that were hiding the shanty. It was well hidden from sight, only being visible from the sky above. The sand dunes surrounded all four sides of the building. Even the small sandy path leading up to the shanty was hidden from view. The existence of the shanty was known to no one other than the three men who were present this evening. Other than the faint sound of dance music from the Disco, that could only be heard on a calm and storm-free night, the shanty provided the seclusion the three men needed.

Jeremy laid Michele down gently on the old mattress covered in moldy stains from other women's bodily fluids and their male bodily fluids. He quickly removed all her clothing, and with the aid of Captain Jack, they used the leather cuffs to bind her tightly to the bed. Both the wrist and ankle cuffs were well-padded to avoid leaving marks from the bindings. If the men needed to get rough with their guests, they always picked spots on the body that would be hidden by clothing. The abdomen and inner thighs were spots they frequently used. The women were always lying on their backs, so the men were careful to never hit them in the midsection. Amburo shoved a gag in Michele's mouth to keep her quiet, then blindfolded her. Just as they finished with the bindings, Michele started to wake up. She had no idea Jeremy had slipped Chloral hydrate, better known as a Mickey, in her drink, knocking her out for less than an hour. She tried to move so she could rub her temples from the headache she had from the drug but could not move her arms or legs. She could not open her eyes or speak, and she began to panic. She tried to struggle to free herself before feeling the striking blow to her head that momentarily dazed her. Finally, Jeremy spoke, "Welcome to the VIP room." Michele did not recognize his voice. Jeremy had placed a small white cylinder on his throat. The electrolarynx altered his voice, making it sound like a monotone electronic buzz. Jeremy spoke slowly, which added to the robotic effect that drove fear into his victims that his past VIP guests and now Michele had become. Out of fear and panic she tried struggling to free herself a second time only to be met with another mind-numbing slap to the side of her head, delivered by Amburo. Michele remained still as she quickly figured out any resistance meant physical harm would follow. She was terrified; she could not see, move, or speak. The robotic voice increased the terror she was feeling. *I don't want to die. Daddy, where are you? Please help me,* Were the thoughts inside her head. The robotic voice told her that if she kept her mouth shut and didn't scream, he would remove the gag. The thing Jeremy loved the most was listening the moans of pleasure from his victims. Those involuntary moans only reinforced his theory that women liked what was being done to them. Their moans of sexual pleasure, and their eventual climax was all the proof he needed to know that they were enjoying themselves. He convinced himself he was giving them the ultimate VIP experience they would never forget. It was true the experience was and will be something his victims would never forget. Sadly, a few of his VIPs had such horrific memories of the experience that it led them to the taking of their own life. The robotic voice asked her if she understood. Michele nodded, "Yes." The voice asked if she was going to scream. She shook her head, "No" letting him know she will obey. Jeremy nodded to Amburo to remove the gag. Amburo grabbed her hair, yanked Michele's head up and untied the gag. Michele fought hard to keep from screaming out in pain caused by the sudden and violent yanking of her hair. Amburo let Michele's head drop back down onto the mattress. In that instant, there was complete silence, no thunder in the distance, and no waves crashing on the shore. Michele let out a furious scream and cried for help as loudly as she possibly could, praying, she could be heard by someone, anyone who could help her. She prayed that her daddy would hear her screaming cries for help. Michele desperately prayed that her daddy, her hero, her savior, would come crashing through the door and liberate her from the bindings that held her captive. Michele envisioned her proverbial knight in shining armor would single-handedly beat down her unknown captors and restrain them by placing the shackles and restraints they used on her to hold them till the police arrived. But none of that happened. Michele's screaming was stopped by Amburo's fist slamming into her abdominal area. The blow was so abrupt and forceful, it instantly knocked the wind out of Michele. The pain was sudden and intense, sending sharp waves of pain through her body. In a dominant and commanding expression, the robotic voice of Captain Jack said, "You stupid cunt! No one can hear you! Now shut the fuck up!" Amburo placed his own electrolarynx to his throat, telling Michele, "Next time you scream I will cut out your tongue." The electrolarynx disguised his voice but could not hide that broad African accent which would haunt Michele for years to come.

Amburo set the device down and replaced the gag with an O-Ring gag. This gag left her mouth wide open, it also left her unable to speak or scream. She could only emit slight moans of pain and discomfort from the punch she took to the gut. Once the gag was firmly in place, all three men stripped naked. Jeremy reached under the bed to retrieve the detachable stirrups and the other toys he kept under there. He attached the stirrups to the lower side rails and untied the bindings that held Michele's legs in place. He tried to force her legs into the stirrups, but once again, Michele tried to fight back by kicking wildly with her now free legs. Michele felt a sharp jolt of pain go through her right temple that immediately stunned her into submission. Jeremy tried using his electrolarynx device to yell, but the limitations of the device would not allow for emotions, which triggered his rage. Jeremy violently slammed Amburo up against the shanty wall with enough force that the tiny building shook on its foundation. Jeremy wrapped his hands tightly around Amburo's throat, squeezing hard enough to restrict Amburo's breathing. Standing nose to nose with Amburo, Jeremy's neck tensed, and in a low, threatening voice through gritted teeth laced with the wrath of God himself said, "How many FUCKING TIMES do I have to tell you! Open hand to the head! No fists to the temple! EVER! You could kill her! Then we are all fucked!" Jeremy's violent outbursts would send fear shivering through the body of whoever was on the receiving end of his of his blind rage. Amburo never forgot the beat down Jeremy gave Captain Jack the first time they both saw Jeremy naked in the shanty. Jack made fun of Jeremy's size which drove Jeremy into one of his blind rages. Amburo stood there, like the once helpless child he was, watching his mother being violently raped and tortured by the militia. Jeremy had beaten Captain Jack so badly he was unable to walk out of the shanty nor stand on his own two feet without help for several days. Captain Jack stood watching with the horror of the one and only time Jeremy attacked him deeply rooted in his memory. He knew better than to try and stop Jeremy, it only took the one attack for the captain to get the message loud and clear. Jeremy let go of Amburo, who kept himself pinned against the wall because of the terrified state he was in. Jeremy's mood and demeanor could cycle instantaneously from calm to a violent rage and back to calm. Jeremy suffered from the undiagnosed condition, folie circulaire sometimes referred to as circular insanity and better known in the medical field as bipolar disorder. It was the disorder that caused him to go from zero to sixty and back again in the blink of an eye. Not knowing which mood was coming next was what terrified both his partners in crime. The thought of telling him "No" or to "Stop" with the rapes they were committing horrified them both. The first time the three of them did this Amburo and Captain Jack had no idea Jeremy had drugged the woman with chloral hydrate. Jeremy told them she was compliant because she loved sex games and was role-playing. He told the two of them there was a safe word. He explained that if she did not say the safe word, then it was all part of the role-play game. It was the following day when the drugs had worn off the woman that they discovered there never was a safe word. It was then that they realized they raped her. It was also then that Captain Jack confronted Jeremy for the first and only time. That was the night Amburo developed a type of victim bonding with the soldiers who abused him and his mother. He was not the reluctant partner in crime that Captain Jack was forced to become. The thought of spending twenty years in a Mexican prison, if a rapist would even survive, was enough for Captain Jack to cave and become one of Jeremy's VIP treatment hosts, as he called it. The uncontrolled and always violent outbursts would give Jeremy an erection. Violence was an aphrodisiac for him; it was a form of foreplay in his warped mind. Jeremy quickly attached the stirrups to the bed and strapped Michele's legs into them before she came to. Climbing between Michele's legs, he inserted himself in her and began raping her. Michele, getting her wits about her, became conscious and aware of her situation again. She thought it was his finger that he slid into her, only to realize she was being raped. She had no memory other than dinner and dancing. The rest was just a blur. Michele's body tensed as panic took over. She was bound tightly and could not move. She tried to close her legs and force whoever was inside of her out but could not. She was helpless, all she could do was lie there and hope they would not kill her, and it would be over soon. Captain Jack knew he needed to start giving Michele the VIP treatment so Jeremy would not violently come after him too. He stripped off his clothes and knelt next to the bed, teasing Michele's nipples with his tongue. Michele responded to his tongue with a slight moan as her nipples became erect. Hearing her moan and feeling her erect nipples on his tongue made Captain Jack feel like he was pleasuring her, and she liked it. It was this thought that made it easier to do what he never wanted or ever intended to do to any of their victims. Captain Jack tilted his head slightly so he could make sure Jeremy saw what he was doing. Jeremy nodded his head in approval and gave him "the wink" which was his signal for Captain Jack to slide his hand down Michele's body. This always excited Jeremy because he knew once Captain Jack hit that magic spot, Michele would tense up, try to arch her back, and thrust her hips into his. Jeremy watched with anticipation as Captain Jack's hand did its thing. Amburo, who was still shaken from the attack, stood there watching. He knew the consequences would be severe if he did not get involved. After removing his clothing, Amburo approached the bound and gagged Michele. Still rattled, he had a difficult time getting an erection. He gently tilted Michele's head, so the O-ring gag was facing him. He found inserting his flaccid phallus into her mouth through the O-ring was easier said than done. Once he felt the warmth and moistness of Michele's mouth, he was able to get semi-erect. just enough so the arduous task became less challenging making it easier to slide himself in. He knew he went too deep and too fast as Michele's gag reflexes kicked in. He quickly slid back out and lost what little stiffness he had. He feared Jeremy's rage if he hurt her again. Jeremy did not see or hear Michele's gagging when he looked up and saw Amburo's limp self. "What's with the droopy dog?" he asked. Amburo smiled in return, cautiously, not saying anything, and started to reinsert himself back in. Like before, once he started feeling the warmth and moistness of her mouth, he got excited. This time he went slower and was amazed that when he went slow, she was able to take all of him in. With her mouth wrapped snuggly around his manhood, he began a gentle rhythm of sliding himself back and forth, never leaving her mouth or pushing deep enough to gag her again. Jeremy refocused his attention on Captain Jack, whose fingers were about to reach their destination. Just as Jeremy anticipated, once those fingers found their mark, Michele reacted accordingly. Her back arched up and her muscles tensed, squeezing Jeremy tight causing him to lose control and let out a loud, "OH FUCK!" as he started to ejaculate inside her. No matter how intense the sex was, the three of them would never forget to use their electrolarynx. They always kept them within reach. Jeremy's body shuttered one last time before he finished and removed himself. He hand gestured to Amburo that it was his turn to fuck Michele. Wasting no time and obeying the hand gesture, Amburo quickly slid himself out of Michele's mouth., wasting no time out of fear of losing his erection, he rushed to position himself in between Michele's legs. Just as he was ready to insert himself into Michele, Jeremy, who was now standing behind him, gave him a hard slap on his ass and whispered in his ear, "Bone that bitch good and hard." Jeremy took his place by Michele's head. Using both hands, he twisted Michele's head so her gagged mouth was facing Captain Jack. He gestured for Captain Jack to slide himself into her mouth. Like Amburo, Captain Jack wasted no time and did as Jeremy said. Jeremy bent over and reached down to Michele's breast, taking over rubbing her breasts and sucking on her still erect nipples. Amburo had slid himself deep inside of Michele, and once he entered her, there was no way he was losing his erection. He was much larger in both length and girth than Jeremy was. He was the biggest Michele had ever experienced. It was the girth alone that caused her to gag at first. Now that he was confident, he was not going to lose his erection, he started doing as Jeremy instructed. He boned her good and hard. Kneeling between her outstretched legs, he reached down, raised her hips off the bed, and pulled Michele tight against him. He slid himself out to the point that only the tip was still inside her, then rammed his hips forward till he was all the way in again. He did this slowly at first, then started picking up the rhythm. It was not long before he was ramming her so hard that there was a loud slapping sound from the flesh of their groins hitting one another. Jeremy loved hearing the slapping sound their flesh was making. It drove him wild, getting him hard again. There was enough room on the bed for him to straddle Michele and slide himself between her breasts. He was still wet from being inside Michele, and the drool from both him and Captain Jack provided ample lubrication for him to squeeze her breasts together and start having intercourse with her breasts. All three men were going at it with such force that they came close to breaking the bed. The single window's shutter was closed when Jeremy had first entered, and the door was shut tight. The air inside had gotten hot and reeked of stale body odor and sex. Adding to that stench was the intense sexual tension from four hot and sweaty occupants. The worn bed springs squeaked, almost squealed from the motion, and the men's loud grunting and groaning filled the air with a wretched noise. Finally, Captain Jack could no longer contain himself, he let out a load groan as he climaxed with the same intensity as the climax from earlier in the day when they were on the bridge of his boat. The loud groans of pleasure coming from Captain Jack's orgasm were all it took for Amburo to start his own. Amburo leaned forward when he came, unintentionally letting out a moan of pleasure in Jeremy's ear. This was the first time any man let out a moan of pleasure in Jeremy's ear. It drove Jeremy wild, exciting him to the point he couldn't hold back or control himself, bringing on an uncontrollable orgasm of his own. What Jeremy lacked in size, he more than made up for in his ability to have multiple orgasms with a large volume exploding onto Michele's face and neck. Captain Jack could see that Jeremy was about to explode and quickly moved out of the way so he would not get soaked too.

The guys had gotten themselves dressed and were standing outside the shanty, each smoking their ceremonial cigar. Captain Jack resecured the door, locking Michele inside. He strained to hear Jeremy, who kept his voice low as he praised him and Amburo for their stellar performance. Usually, the session lasts much longer, and tonight would have too, but Jeremy was not expecting Patty and Blake to show up at the Disco. They ended up staying longer than normal and did not have as much time as they wanted to work over Michele. Jeremy gave instructions for Amburo to stop back at the shanty before he makes his first airport run to check in on their "VIP guest". He told Captain Jack to check on her by midday to make sure she got some water and to clean up any messes. With that, he slapped both guys on their backs as they made their way through the sand dunes.

Chapter 16

Michele had no memory of how she got there, where she was, or even who had tied her to the bed. Her mind was racing; she had no memory of that entire evening. Her head was filled with thoughts that left her terrified she was going to be tortured and killed. The robotic voices drove the fear of a horrifically torturous death deeper into her mind. One of the robotic voices said they would remove the gag if she didn't scream. In her state of terror, unable to process a rational thought, she nodded yes, that she understood. Not wanting to die, she obeyed him out of survival instinct alone. Once the gag was removed, there was an immediate eerie calm in the room, there was a dead silence in the air. In her mind Michele's only thought was this was the moment she was going to die. She started screaming with everything she had. Her screaming came to an abrupt stop as massive pain from a driving force pushed all the air out of her body, leaving her desperately gasping for air. She couldn't comprehend what was being said by the robotic voice that was speaking to her. The sharp pain in her abdomen violently radiated through her body, and at that moment it was all she could focus on. The second robotic voice was also incomprehensible, but the accent was the thing that her mind picked up on and was immediately deeply rooted into her psyche. In those moments of intense pain, the only thing she realized was her mouth would not close because the strap that now wrapped around her head was forcing her mouth to remain open.

Her mind was acting without conscious thought, driving itself deeper into survival mode. It was doing everything it could out of fear to fight the brutal abuse and violation of her body. Michele had just enough of her wits about her to feel the release of her legs from their bindings. Again, without thought or rationality, she began kicking her legs wildly trying to free herself and escape. She felt a sudden blow to her head, causing her mind to go dark and her body to go limp. Michele was out cold. She had no idea there was an altercation that shook the walls of the shanty happening right next to her. As she started to come too, she couldn't move her legs again. She felt the bed shake as Jeremy crawled between her legs. At first it felt as if a finger was being inserted into her but soon realized he was inside her when his pelvic area started to slap against hers. She then felt her nipples start to become erect as someone sucked on one while rubbing and teasing the other, causing her to moan with pleasure. As the helpless Michele lay there on the bed, she started gagging from the large thing being shoved into her mouth. She thought for sure her gagging would cause her to get hit again and began bracing herself for the impact that never came. This time, there was no impact or pain in her temple before she passed out. This time, she felt the large object slide out. When her gagging ceased, she could feel the object gently sliding back in her mouth. As the object was sliding back in her mouth, she recognized it was a man's penis. Now knowing what it was, she relaxed and let the man slide his penis in her mouth. Michele had always had uncontrollable nymphomaniac tendencies, which was something she discovered after her first experience with her cousin. Ever since then, she couldn't get enough sex to fill her furious and never-ending sexual appetite. She liked to experiment with different types of kink from time to time, and tonight, it was those nymphomaniac tendencies that became the tool for her survival. Michele, in a brief moment of clarity, was fully aware that she was being brutally raped. Her subconscious mind, jumping into survival mode, started to kick in the sexual pleasure receptors in her brain to protect her mind from the barbaric situation she was in. Michele could feel a hand sliding down her belly, stopping at the top of her clitoral region. She felt a sensation that was heightened by the penis that was sliding in and out of her, the attention her breasts were getting and the erect penis in her mouth. She always enjoyed those sensations, but this was her first experience of having three different men pleasuring her at the same time. The knowledge of being raped had faded and given way to the delight of the sexual ecstasy she was experiencing. Michele's mind was completely lost in the moment and the different sensations happening to the various areas of her body. It was her subconscious mind that had mentally transported her back to the bedroom in the resort where she was doing the thing she had come here to do; have sex with multiple guys at once. Her psyche was deep rooted in the fantasy it had created.

The moaning and grunts coming from Michele were the positive reinforcement the three men wanted to hear. Michele could feel both men that were inside her going faster and deeper the louder she moaned. When she felt the fingers that were massaging her went slightly further down hitting the spot that caused her to arch her back and with a muffled cry, she started to orgasm with a fierce intensity she hadn't felt before. Having sex with Josh, her cousin, and the night in the van with the twins was what she considered good sex and always drove her to an orgasm, never once having to fake it. As good as her past sexual experiences and climaxes were, this by far had them all beat. It was as if you rolled them all into one massive orgasm and supercharged it. Even though she had the O-ring gag in and Amburo deep in her mouth, she kept letting out muffled screams as she felt the man who was fucking her cum inside her. Her hypersexuality was increasing her carnal pleasure, adding to her psyche's mental defenses that were blocking out the atrocity that was happening to her. Once she and the man who was inside her were done, she felt the bed move as he got out from between her legs. She felt the man in her mouth withdraw, and a moment later the bed shook as someone else was now between her legs and sliding himself in her. At first, Michele tried to squeeze her vaginal muscles in an attempt to keep this other man from penetrating her but soon relaxed and gave way to the pleasure of his enormous manhood. Once he was all the way in, she squeezed again; never had she felt a man this large inside of her before. She was squeezing because she didn't want him to take it out. Her raw, animalistic, and uninhibited desires took over. She was in a feral state, a level of primal sexual instinct she had never achieved before. Her psyche had taken her survival mode into overdrive. Being lost in fantasy, Michele gave no struggle to Captain Jack as he started sliding himself in and out of her mouth. She felt someone straddling her midsection and her breasts were being squeezed together as Jeremy was having sex with her breasts. What her subconscious was doing was working. Michele was lost in the utopian fantasy. The thoughts of being raped, the brutal blows to her body, and the thought of her dying at the hands of her captors were replaced with the artificial fantasy her psyche created. Her bindings were part of the kink in the fantasy, and she was no longer in the reality of what was happening; everything was completely blocked out. With only the thought of sexual gratification drugging her powerless mind, she eagerly accepted both men inside her. Her moans of pleasure were clearly audible as all three men forcibly performed sex acts on her. The only part of her body she could move was her head. She was matching her captor's thrusting motion with her head as she greedily slobbered his engorged manhood. Michele was trying to use her midsection to match the ramming action happening down below. The stirrups that bound her legs were not allowing her to move her midsection, but that didn't stop Michele from trying. She was able to tense and flex her muscles allowing her to squeeze the colossal-sized man that was plunging in and out of her. The squeezing was something the man at the receiving end didn't expect. The tightening around him was adding to his pleasure. The heated passion that filled the shanty had reached its climax. No longer able to hold back, Captain Jack was the first to start releasing what he had been trying hard to hold back. As he exploded into Michele's mouth, she passionately welcomed and savored the hot liquid. Amburo saw his friend climaxing, and with the sounds of his grunting and gasping with pleasure, it caused him to start his own release. Michele felt the eruptive force of his ejaculation that matched the size and robotic cries of his intense orgasm. Having the two of them release their bodily fluids in her at the same time was something Michele had never experienced before. For Michele, it was a sexual euphoria she had not achieved before driving her into one of if not the most powerful orgasms she had ever experienced since becoming sexually active. Her entire body tensed as her skene glands expelled fluid with enough pressure to cause the pubic area of Amburo to be soaked with her juices. Jeremy's body started to tense just as Captain Jack was finishing. Seeing this, Captain Jack knew Jeremy was what they called a "heavy cummer" and saw that he was ready to unleash. He backed away so he wouldn't get sprayed by Jeremy. Jeremy started pumping his hips faster as his chicken bone-sized organ erupted, hitting Michele in the face. Her mouth, still held open with the O-ring gag, became the recipient of his fluid. Michele welcomed the taste of the semen, which she quickly grew to enjoy.

When all was finally said and done, and the men dismounted the bed, she lay there with that still drugged-out euphoric feeling from the powerful endorphins her pituitary gland had pumped into her system.

The state she was in caused her to give no resistance as Amburo, who was the first to finish cleaning up and getting dressed, replaced the O-ring with the original cloth gag they used on her. Nor did she give resistance when he unbound her from the stirrups and re-bound her with the padded leather straps, then double checked her wrist restraints. After a while, the endorphins began to wear off, and Michele's conscious mind brought her situation back into focus. Michele's mind was now filled with thoughts of her being murdered, once again causing the panic to dominate. *Where am I? What is happening? What have they done to me? DADDY! Help me, they're going to kill me!* were the thoughts invading her cerebrum causing her to feel sheer terror. She started thrashing, trying to escape the confines that held her firmly to the bed. Her head was thrashing from side to side when she felt a heavy weight pressing down on her chest to limit her tossing around. She felt a prick on her arm followed by a slight burning sensation from the sedative Amburo was injecting into her. Within seconds, her head started to spin. As her thoughts were getting fuzzy, Michele tried to fight and stay awake, but the drug won. Michele drifted into the darkness of nothingness and the deep sleep brought on by the drug.

Chapter 17

The next morning, Patty was beginning to stir in bed as she started her typical ritual of stretching, yawning, and slowly waking up while still wrapped in Blake's arms. Patty was groggy, not fully awake, as she envisioned herself wrapped tightly in the arms of Josh, not Blake. Enjoying the delusion of the semi-dream-like state her mind was in, Patty started rubbing Blake's chest as it gently rose up and down with his breathing. Gently rubbing and slowly sliding her hand lower, she started running her finger through the lines of his six-pack abs, then continued to the targeted destination. Still asleep, Blake instinctively spread his legs enough to allow Patty to explore between them. She tossed the covers aside, exposing Blake, and shifted between his legs so she could take him in her mouth. Blake's flaccid male organ quickly reacted to the warm and wet sensation of Patty's mouth. He, started to wake up, and began moaning with pleasure at Patty's bobbing up and down on him. With one hand, she started caressing his swollen rocks. The other hand wrapped around his shaft and with a firm grip started stroking up and down with the same rhythm as her mouth. Blake, now fully awake and aware of what Patty was doing, arched his back and hips to match Patty's motions. The bedroom was filled with groaning and grunting from Blake as he shouted to the great deity in the sky. His hands were clenching the sheets, trying to hold back as long as he could. Unable to hold back any longer, he lifted his head and looking down at Patty, he shouted, "OH GOD I can't hold back I'm gonna nut!" Patty was lost in the fantasy of being with Josh instead of Blake as she eagerly took him to completion.

They both were lying back in bed trying to catch their breath and basking in the afterglow of their morning romp before realizing the time. Blake knew he had just an hour to go back to his place, gather his things, and get to the lifeguard station. Patty rolled out of bed and went straight for the shower. She stood in the shower, allowing the warmth of the soothing water to gently rinse away the lingering scent of last night's and their early morning escapade. As hunger pains began to take over, Patty reluctantly decided it was time to turn the water off, after the longest shower of her life, so she could order breakfast. Wrapping herself in the fluffy white robe the hotel provided for all their guests, she headed to the living room to order room service. Stopping at Michele's bedroom door, she was hesitant at first to knock and ask Michele if she wanted breakfast too, thinking to herself that she probably had an overnight guest in there. Patty decided to knock anyway, and when there was no answer, she knocked a second and third time. Still no answer. She slowly cracked the door open, calling her name and keeping her head turned so she wouldn't see anything if she was in there. Still, there was no answer, she turned her head to investigate the silent bedroom, only to find the bed had not been slept in, nor was anyone in the room. She was thinking to herself, *someone didn't come home last night, no surprise there,* as she walked back to the phone and ordered room service for one. Patty had gotten dressed and was on the balcony when room service knocked at the door with her breakfast order.

When Mateo arrived at work on the morning Patty discovered Michele's empty bedroom, Jeremy was also among the missing. Mateo always waited by the time clock for Jeremy so he and his best friend at work could clock in together. Mateo's mother saw him waiting by the time clock and knew he wasn't aware that Jeremy had called out sick that morning. She walked over to tell Mateo that Jeremy wouldn't be in today. Upon hearing the news from his mother, the uneasy feeling in his stomach, along with the sense that something was wrong grew inside him again. He couldn't get his mind off the blonde girl with the big boobs. He wasn't infatuated with or lusting for Michele, it was genuine concern he had for her. He was afraid for her, he didn't know why he felt that way he just did. He was also worried for Jeremy who had never called in sick or missed a day of work. When he got to his normal bellhop station, he was asked by the front desk staff to take the room service cart to a guest's room while he waited for the airport limo to arrive with new guests. Mateo was eager to take the cart after seeing which room it was going to because he was able to make sure the pretty blonde girl was okay. He took a breath before gently knocking on the door and announcing, "room service." Patty opened the door and was greeted by a visibly anxious Mateo. She let him in and asked him to leave the cart next to the sliding glass door that led to the balcony. Even though Mateo had the cognitive ability of a third grader, he could be quick on his feet with his thinking especially when he felt it was of the utmost importance. He said to Patty, "The kitchen must have made a mistake, I only see one plate of food. I will go and get the rest of your order right away." He knew the kitchen didn't make a mistake and thought this would be a good way for him to find out where the blonde girl with the big boobs was without having to come out and ask for her. Patty told him there was no mistake, Michele wasn't there, and she must have spent the night with Jeremy. Mateo's concern grew. His best friend at work called out sick, and the girl with the big boobs didn't return. He didn't let his concern show on his face as his training taught him. The hotel management trained their employees well to deliver friendly, personalized, and exceptional service to all the resort's guests. Mateo did, or at least made the attempt to, do the best he could to deliver excellent service. He didn't understand why, but he did know how important it was because that is how he got big tips. He told Patty that if she needed anything else, please let him or any hotel staff know, and they would be happy to assist her. Then he showed himself to the door. Once outside in the empty hallway, he let his concern and worry show as he hurried back to his station.

Patty sat enjoying her breakfast on the balcony as she gazed at the beach and the Caribbean Sea while enjoying some alone time. Patty loved Michele like a sister, even idolized her, however, the solitude was a nice change of pace. This peaceful moment gave her time to think about Josh and how much she wanted to be with him. She was looking out onto the beach when she saw Blake heading to the lifeguard shack. She really enjoyed their date and of course, the fun they had in bed together. She thought she would feel guilty about being with him because of her wanting to save herself for Josh. Realizing she didn't feel guilty because she was thinking about Josh the whole time, and since there was no intercourse, she was still a virgin. Even though Patty knew when the trip was over, she would never see him again, she had developed feelings for Blake. Patty admitted to herself, she really did like Blake and wanted to be with him as much as she wanted Josh, even though she had just the one date. There was something about Blake that made her feel special, the same way Josh made her feel special, even though she and Josh were not together. Looking out at the beach, she saw him waving to her as he unlocked the shack door and set the day's water conditions flag out. She knew she should stop by the shack and say Hi, as she thought to herself, *why bother to come up with a reason to see him? Just do it.* Happy with that thought, she went back to her room, changed into her bikini, and left for the beach. On her way down, she stopped at Mateo's station to let him know the room service cart was ready to be picked up, and if he saw Michele, let her know that she was going to be on the beach and to join her if she wanted. Patty again noticed there was something off with Mateo today. Even so, he happily agreed to give Michele the message and take care of the cart for her.

She got the same feeling, just like she had when she opened the door for him earlier when he delivered the room service cart. Patty was quick to pick up on the anxiety. She hoped nothing was wrong because she really liked Mateo; he was one of those people that you just couldn't help but like. He was always smiling and loved to be of service to the guests. Both Patty and Michele always made sure they tipped him well. For some strange reason, Patty couldn't shake the feeling something was wrong as she walked out of the resort and onto the beach. She still couldn't get Mateo off her mind or shake that strange feeling she had when she got to the lifeguard shack.

Blake saw Patty coming across the beach and could tell, even from the hundred-foot distance that was between them, she was lost in thought. He could tell something was weighing on her mind. They were happy to see one another, and they put their arms around each other's waist without hesitation and kissed. They tightened their embrace, matching the deep passion of their kissing. It was clear that Blake was having the same unspoken feelings towards Patty that she was having for him. Releasing their lip lock but still embracing, Blake asked what was on her mind. Patty hesitated to reply; she was not only trying to find the right words, but she was also thinking she was concerned over nothing. She finally responded by saying it was nothing; she was just being silly. Blake wasn't buying it; he knew something was bothering her. Giving her a supportive squeeze, he told her she was not being silly and asked again. Patty reluctantly told Blake about Mateo and how she picked up on his anxiety and about Michele not coming back from her date. She told him how she was just brushing both things off as a coincidence, till she walked by the pool bar and didn't see Jeremy. Telling Blake was when her concern grew. Jeremy bragged about never missing work, and even though they had only been there a few days, she noticed Jeremy was always at the pool bar doing his thing. Not seeing him there after Michele had told her she wouldn't be too late cause Jeremy had to work the next morning, gave her a creepy feeling. Patty again said she knew she was just being silly and added, "they're probably still in bed, and knowing Michele, she is wearing the poor guy out." Blake gave her another supportive squeeze thinking to himself he needed to check on Mateo to see if he could find out what was bothering him. Since he saw who was with Jeremy last night at the Disco, he wanted to see if the other two were MIA. This didn't feel right to him either. He had heard the rumors at the Disco that on occasion, female patrons from the resort, especially the ones traveling alone or with other females who were not traveling with male companions, would go missing. He had no proof that this was happening, just hearsay rumors. Hearing this from Patty made him wonder if the rumors had some truth to them. Blake thought that Patty thinking they were still sleeping or having sex, was the more rational explanation. He reassured Patty that she wasn't being silly, and he would be happy to check in on Mateo. That made Patty feel better, not great, but better. She asked if she could hang out with him for a while. Blake was happy to let Patty hang out, especially if it helped ease her mind. From his Lifeguard shack, with the aid of his binoculars, he could check to see the comings and goings of Captain Jack's boat. This is what he did as he was making scans of the water, checking on the safety of the swimmers who were sparsely populating the off-season beach. It took a while, but he did see Captain Jack's boat heading out to the reef for a snorkeling trip. Around noon time, his relief came, so he could take a lunch break. He and Patty went to the resort's beach grill to grab a couple of their self-proclaimed "famous beach burgers" and fries for lunch. With the excuse of needing the restroom, Blake was able to check to see if Amburo had shown up to work. As luck would have it, Amburo had arrived at work as normal and was at the driver's station getting the flight arrival information and guests' names he was picking up at the airport on his first run of the day. Without making his presence known, Blake headed back to Patty, feeling better about the situation. Needing to use the restroom was more than just an excuse to check to see if Amburo had shown up to work. As he was walking out of the restroom, Mateo was coming down the same corridor with an empty luggage cart heading back to his station. Blake greeted Mateo and asked how he was doing today. Right away, Blake picked up on what Patty was talking about. Something was off with Mateo today. Blake kept the conversation superficial and brief, knowing Mateo needed to get back to his station. They quickly parted ways, and Blake was back at the table just as their burgers and fries were being served. When they finished their lunch, Blake told Patty he needed to get back to the lifeguard shack. He told her she was welcome to hang out there till his shift ended at four that afternoon. She declined, saying she was feeling better and wanted to souvenir shop at a few of the shops around the resort. Blake asked if she wanted dinner again tonight. Patty didn't even have to think about it, she said yes with no hesitation.

Blake was once again scanning the water keeping an eye on the few beach goers that were enjoying the water. He spotted Captain Jack's boat coming back from its earlier trip out to the reef but gave no more thought to it since it was nothing out of the ordinary. The afternoon was uneventful as it usually is during off-season and as his shift ended, Blake was quick to call it a day; he was excited to see Patty again tonight.

Patty found some handmade purses made from colorful fabric for her mother. She came across a sombrero that had a T-shirt sold with it. The T-shirt had a colorful graphic on it that said, "My daughter went to Cancun and all I got was this lousy sombrero." She laughed out loud when she read the shirt, thinking that it would be perfect for her father. She could picture him wearing the T-shirt and sombrero to Sunday service. Then she thought about how she hated that church group they belonged to; it felt like a cult. She promised her future self that she and Josh were not going to raise their kids in that group. She wrapped up her shopping and headed back to the resort to check and see if Michele had returned.

Chapter 18

The sun cast a red glow on the Caribbean Sea as it began to rise, marking the beginning of a new day. The day was just starting when Amburo arrived at the shanty. It was well before his first airport run of the day, he was checking on Michele like he usually does when they have VIP guests at the shanty. Looking at the sun-faded "VIP guests only" sign that Jeremy had hung on the door, he thought to himself *VIP guests, how the hell did he come up with that?* After a slight snort which was meant to be a slight chuckle, Amburo unlocked the shanty door and stepped inside. He looked down at the bed, and it was like a switch flicked in his mind. He now saw himself as one of the cruel and sadistic soldiers who had repeatedly raped his mother. In his mind he was no longer the weak, helpless child he was back in Africa. He is now a strong man who is no longer the child who hid because he was too afraid of the soldiers to protect his mother. He felt the rage of a sadistic rapist begin to boil up inside him. He said out loud what he thought was only said in his head. "I don't know why whores like you always resist. Dis is what you were put on this earth for. Dis is what happens when you resist and not do what you are supposed to do." Michele wasn't awake enough to hear and understand the words; her mind was in a drug-induced fog. Through the haziness of the dream-like state she was in, the only thing she could make out was a male voice with a deep accent. In her confused drug-induced state she had no idea who it was or where the accent was from. The only thing she knew was that this was one of her night terrors that seemed all too real. She was stuck in this horrible nightmare, this night terror that she couldn't wake up from. Amburo saw Michele's head start to roll back and forth and knew the drugs were wearing off. He knew that from this point on, no more talking unless he used his electrolarynx to disguise his voice. He had a policeman's billy club in his hand, and he gave her a quick sharp blow across her abdomen. Not hard enough to cause internal damage, yet hard enough to get the message across, which was, this is going to be brutal. In her drug-induced state, she barely flinched at the blow, but the pain registered in her mind loud and clear. The robotic voice instructed her to remain silent and do not try anything because there was no one there to save her this time. Michele knew she needed to be obedient and gave no trouble as Amburo released her legs from the restraints. Amburo had taken the stirrups out from under the bed and attached them both to the bed's side rails on the same side of the bed. He undid the binding on Michele's right arm and slid her around so that one arm was bound to the top and the other arm bound at the bottom. He bound her legs in the stirrups so that she was in a spread-eagle position. He stripped down and was now standing between her legs naked and erect while gently rubbing the end of his billy club on her belly. The billy club was the type that had a rounded handle coming out the side with a rounded end that resembled a mushroom. Police men would grab the handle and hold the billy-club so that it would run the length of their forearm to help protect them from an assault. Amburo had other plans for the handle. The girth of the billy club and its handle was slightly larger than the girth of his erect penis. Michele laid there with the blindfold and gag still doing their job. As the drug was wearing off the tears were building up behind the blindfold. Fear was starting to take over, and she knew she was going to get raped again. Her mind started screaming, "WAKE UP! JUST WAKE THE FUCK UP! OH GOD JUST WAKE UP!" Her mind's screaming quickly turned into whimpering and begging. "Please just wake up and it will stop. I just want it to stop. Daddy, please wake me up." As hard as she pleaded with herself and as hard as Michele tried, she couldn't wake up from the night terror she was convinced she was having. There was no way this could be happening. Not to her and not in real life. She tried to convince herself it was just a night terror that no matter how hard she tried she couldn't wake up from. Amburo started tapping Michele's stomach with rapid repetitions of the billy club that caused Michele to refocus her attention back to him. He could tell her mind wasn't focused on him and knew the tapping would get her to pay attention. Using the electrolarynx he spoke in his robotic voice, "There is no one here to stop me. One wrong move and it will be your last." Just because Jeremy wasn't there didn't mean Amburo could do anything he wanted. He knew Jeremy would find out and it would be a beating he knew he wouldn't survive. But Michele didn't know that, and he knew it would strike fear in her. He knew for that brief time, he was the dominant one who held control over her. Amburo dipped the mushroom head of the handle into the sex lube jar that was part of the box Jeremy kept under the bed. He knelt between her legs and started rubbing the tip of the handle on the outer folds of her vaginal lips. Michele was intimidated to the point that she was terrified by the threat Amburo had just made. The rubbing of her vagina normally would have sent her right into seventh heaven but because of the terror that had just been instilled in her, it caused the fondling to barely register in her mind. Amburo kept rubbing the end of the handle of the billy club in her which was giving him more pleasure than it was giving Michele. He dipped his free hand into the lube then started pleasuring himself, gently stroking, matching the rhythm of the billy club handle. He kept this going till he unintentionally hit Michele's magic spot, causing her to arch her back and let out a moan of pleasure. Amburo immediately stopped pleasuring himself at the sound of her groan. Knowing that would cause him to lose control and release what had been building up, he let go of himself. He took a few deep breaths to regain control over himself. Once he did, he was ready to continue. He took the end of the handle and started to slide it inside of Michele. Hitting her spot was all it took for the terror to subside and for her mind to go into protection mode. As she felt the hard plastic handle slide into her, Michele's mind started to drift from the reality that was going on to the time her and Josh were parked down by the creek in his AMC Pacer. The deeper

Amburo slid the hard plastic handle into her, the further her mind drifted into the fantasy till she was no longer aware of her surroundings. With her psyche taking over and protecting her mentally, the fantasy became vivid in her mind's eye. She could see herself sitting next to Josh in his car, which was parked in a secluded area just off the narrow dirt road that led to the creek. The area around the creek was overgrown with thick brush that had taken over the picnic grounds, which was formally a local gathering place for the town. The town was nothing more than a small village back in the early part of the century. Back in its heyday, the villagers would gather at the picnic grounds by the creek for summertime celebrations and picnics. You could always count on fireworks on the Fourth of July. After World War 2 when the soldiers arrived home from war the baby boom began, and it didn't take very long for the tiny village to grow into a small town that quickly outgrew the picnic grounds at the creek. The villagers started gathering over at the State Park at Lake George located just north of Sherman's Corner on the Belfast Augusta Road. The old creek picnic area was soon forgotten, leaving the abandoned area to overgrow. It was in the late sixties that the area would be rediscovered by the local teenagers looking for a place to park where they could smoke pot, have sex, and not get busted. The place was the best kept secret in town because no one besides horny teenagers would go there. It was the same park that Michele was conceived in. Most nights they would get out of his car and either take a stroll down to the water's edge or do it right there on the hood of Josh's car. The night she was fantasizing about was a rainy night. There were numerous times they had sex, but that night was the first time inside his car and the first time Michele showed Josh her deviant side. Josh had carefully set the parking brake and made sure the car was still in gear so it wouldn't roll away like he always did. Sex in the car proved to be awkward for the young teenagers since it was the first time they tried it; they didn't realize that the back seat folded down, making it easier to stretch out. Josh's car had front bucket seats that reclined. They were both leaning over the center console in a deep lip lock when Josh reached for the lever to recline his seat and gently pulled Michele on top of him. By this time, Josh's gym shorts were around his ankles and Michele's mini skirt was on the passenger side floor next to her panties. Michele was trying to get over to Josh's side so she could lie on top of him but ended up straddling the center console. She tried to push herself up so she could swing her other leg over the console but ended up jamming the stick shift into her crotch. Josh had replaced the factory knob with one of those eightball-style shifter knobs. As she was squirming around, she let out a slight moan of pleasure as the knob kept rubbing against her crotch. Josh heard the moan and looked down to see where the knob was. Smiling, he said, "I double dare you to stick the gear shift in your pussy." Michele gave an evil grin and wiggled herself into a better position and slid the knob into her like Josh had dared her to. The vision in her mind's eye of what happened that night began to align with what Amburo was doing. Amburo now had the billy club handle deep inside Michele. He had a strong grip on the shaft of it and a hand on each side of the handle. The anger and rage building inside him could be seen in his eyes: mentally he was no longer in the same room. He was envisioning himself as the soldier who had raped his mother with his rifle. His breathing was becoming fierce and labored, and through his gritted teeth, spittle was spewing out of his mouth with every exhale. He started ramming the handle in and out of Michele with deep, hard thrusts, causing her severe pain. The pain had started altering the fantasy Michele's subconscious mind put her in. Quickly fading from her mind was the excitement of the wild sexual escapades of two horny teenagers--The fantasy of the night they both discovered how much they enjoyed taking a walk on the kinky side and proved there was more to sex than just intercourse. Now, the dream was replaced with her yelling in her mind for Josh to stop, letting him know the knob from the shifter was hurting her. In her vision, tears were running down her cheeks as she again cried out in pain. Her neck was arched back with her head whipping back and forth on the pillow, the pain was too much for her mind to bare. Her own psyche couldn't protect her any longer. Michele bit down on the gag as hard as she could and let out a scream from deep within her while her head continued whipping back and forth. Suddenly, every muscle in her body tensed. It was as if she was frozen solid. Her back had arched up, and she looked as if she was in a state of suspended animation. Then suddenly her entire body went limp. The mind's vision of the fantasy; gone, now replaced with an empty state of blackness. Her last and only defense was for her mind to shut down and send her into the bottomless abyss of nothing. No feeling, no emotion, no awareness, just nothing, she was gone.

Amburo's mind was still gone to that place where the trauma of his childhood had repeatedly taken place time and time again. The years of watching his mother's torture, forever etched in the deepest part of his cerebral cortex. What would bring him back to reality were the cries of the little boy hunched in a dark corner of the tiny hut, rocking back and forth in the fetal position, begging the soldiers to stop hurting his mommy. Seeing himself and hearing his own voice snapped him back to the present. His breathing was now less fierce and labored as he grew more aware of where he was. Aware and present in the reality of the shanty, he looked down and saw the horror of what he was doing. He saw the instant bruises and the blood-stained handle that was caused by him. He was frightened by the lifeless body that lay in front of him. Amburo knew he took it too far. Like many times in the past when he was alone with their victims, he only wanted to physically overpower and dominate them. He wanted those, as he would call them, "dirty whores" to fear him. This was the first time he killed someone. Not knowing what else to do, he quickly removed Michele from the stirrups and repositioned her just like he had left her the night before. He put the stirrups back right where he found them after he bound her to the bed. The handle of the billy club was covered in the sex lube that Amburo used, and Michele's bodily fluids making it appear bloodier than it was. He used his own shirt to wipe clean the evidence of what he had done from Michele's body. Jeremy would notice if the tiniest speck was out of place. Knowing Jeremy had a compulsion to make sure everything was where it should be, Amburo worked frantically to make sure he got everything put back just as he found it. Taking a final look at Michele and making sure she looked like he didn't do anything to her, he picked up the billy club and his shirt and headed for the door.

The eye peering up through the knothole in the floor of the shanty closed. The owner of the peering eye was lying down behind the center pillar that held up the floor, hiding from view. He didn't want Amburo to see him, nor did he want Amburo to know there was an eyewitness to what had just happened.

Chapter 19

Captain Jack finished docking his boat from his morning tour and headed to the shanty to get Michele ready for later that evening. He arrived a little later than expected. Jeremy knew he had a morning tour and knowing that eased Captain Jack's mind. He knew Jeremy wouldn't be upset if he was a little late with the chore at hand. Like he always did, Captain Jack went the back way through the sand dunes to ensure no one would see him. He arrived at the shanty in the opposite direction that Amburo left in. Immediately, he noticed the sand on the back side of the shanty was disturbed. It appeared as if someone had crawled under the shanty. Seeing this, he knew he had to check it out. Mexico was noted for its lack of protection and penalties for rapists on the federal level. Mexico was also noted for allowing the individual states, like Quintana Roo, the state Cancun is in, to have their own criminal codes and definitions of rape. This allowed the state of Quintana Roo to implement strict laws and harsh punishments for anyone who was found guilty of raping tourists. Captain Jack was aware of this making it the last thing he wanted: to be caught and end up in a Mexican prison for the rest of his life. He would rather risk a potentially deadly beating from Jeremy than spend any amount of time in a Mexican prison. After taking a closer look and finding no one under the shanty, he went to check the door and Michele. He found the door and the lock just as they left them night before. He went inside to see that Michele was still there and in the same position as they left her. Since everything was as they left it, and he was completely unaware of what Amburo had done on his morning visit, he assumed it must have been a sea turtle laying her eggs under the shanty. He set his duffle bag down, which contained his usual gear that consisted of a bucket, washcloth, soap, towels, a douche and a few jugs of water. Michele was still out of it from the drug she was given the night before, so he thought anyway. Figuring the drugs would be wearing off soon, he quickly began giving Michele a sponge bath. He removed the soiled gag that was in her mouth so he could wash the dried and crusty body fluids from Jeremy's (as he would say) "titty session" from her face and neck. He replaced the gag with a fresh clean one, then continued down to her breasts to clean up the dried lubricant. He thought to himself, *Man, he loves to titty fuck these girls.* Captain Jack loved her large breasts and noted how firm they were for their size. He wanted to play with them and suck on her nipples but the thought of what Jeremy had done last night put the kibosh on that idea. After cleaning up her midsection, it was time to give his favorite part of a woman a good cleaning. He noticed the bruising around her vagina and lower pelvic area. Seeing this raised an eyebrow of concern. He didn't remember either Jeremy or Amburo being any more aggressive than normal. He gave Michele a closer look and noticed a few tiny drops of dried blood on her. There was some on the mattress too, but he wasn't sure if that was from her. He cleaned her up both inside and out and saw no other traces of blood, figuring the blood was from last night's rough play, and quickly wrapped up his chore. Looking down at a now cleaned-up Michele, he finally took notice of just how limp and lifeless she was. He felt her body and she was almost cool to the touch. He could have sworn she was breathing when he put the clean gag in her mouth. He started to panic and his mind raced with thoughts of how to get rid of the body. How can they cover this up without getting caught? There were too many people who saw her with Jeremy last night, and he knew Jeremy wouldn't, as they say, "go down alone" for her murder. Trying to remain calm and think clearly, he took several deep breaths. With his thoughts now being slightly more rational, he loosened the gag to see if he could feel and hear her breathing. He leaned in to get closer to her mouth with his ear and tilted his head to see if her chest was rising up and down. The sound of her breathing was faint, and her chest was barely moving up and down. Captain Jack breathed a sigh of relief finding that she was still alive. He replaced the gag and took a step back. He picked up the jug of water and started splashing the water on her face attempting to wake her up. It took several attempts, but she eventually started to stir and wake up. Captain Jack sat on the edge of the bed giving her a good once-over with his eyes to make sure she was okay. After staring at her naked body for few minutes, all the panic and irrational thoughts were gone. Those thoughts were now replaced with the lustful thoughts of last evening. The thoughts that were dominating his mind made him want to stay, but he was reluctant to act on them because of how out of it she was. Erring on the side of caution, he decided to leave.

Captain Jack packed up his duffle bag and headed for the door. Glancing back at Michele just before walking out the door and not being able to take his eyes off her, he stood there lusting and staring. Seeing her fully exposed was causing a stirring in his pants he could no longer ignore. He dropped the duffle bag and walked back over to her unable to resist, he unbound her legs, slid his shorts off and climbed in between her legs. Even though Michele was awake, her mind was still shut down, and her body, limp. Michele had no fight in her. She didn't resist when Captain Jack spread her legs wide open and started to insert himself in her. She had no idea she was being raped again, nothing was registering in her mind. Captain Jack was kneeling on the bed with his hands underneath Michele lifting the small of her back up enough so he could do his thing. He was fucking her so hard that the clapping sound their bodies were making echoed off the bare walls of the shanty. This was nothing like what they did on his boat, he much preferred when they either struggled to get free or got into it as much as he did. He was enjoying it, nonetheless. He could feel his nads tightening up and the climax built up in his body. He pumped harder into her as the tension in his body grew. He was doing everything he could to hold it back, wanting it to last longer. The pressure had grown to the point he couldn't hold back, and he started to burst, letting out a roar of, "OH MY

FUCKING GOD!" He was thrusting even faster and ramming her harder with every thrust till he was empty. Completely spent, he was on all fours leaning over her, panting and trying to catch his breath as the sweat from his forehead dribbled onto her belly. It was at this moment he realized he didn't use his electrolarynx. He knew he screwed up and screwed up badly. Back in panic mode, and without thinking, he grabbed his duffle bag and started cleaning her up again. When he went to place her legs back into the bindings, he noticed just how limp she still was. He gently lifted her leg, then let go, watching it drop to the bed. He tried again, getting the same results. Curiously, he called her name, this time using the electrolarynx. He got no response. He moved to the head of the bed, removed her gag, and asked if she could hear him. Still nothing. Although he knew it was wrong and knew better than to do it, he lifted her blindfold to check her eyes. He used his fingers to open her eyelids and saw that she was staring blankly at the ceiling. She didn't blink or react to her name; it was like she was catatonic. He put the blind fold back into place along with the gag and bound her legs to the bed. He was convinced the drugs did this to her and was now sure she didn't even know he was raping her no less heard his voice. Once again, relieved, he got dressed and headed for the door, this time making haste to his exit.

Captain Jack relocked the shanty door and headed back through the sand dunes to his boat, knowing he needed to tell Amburo to lighten up on the drugs. He made a mental note to make sure he told Amburo before Jeremy found out. Knowing he had a few hours before meeting the others at the shanty, he decided to see if he could track down Amburo. God only knew what Jeremy would do to Amburo if he found out just how out of it Michele was from the drugs. Captain Jack carelessly threw the duffle bag onto the boat as he rushed off to find Amburo. He entered from the back alleyway to avoid being seen by hotel management when he arrived at the valet parking area where the hotel drivers would park their Lincoln Town Cars in between runs. This is where you would normally find Ambro when not out on an airport run. He saw Amburo's car but no Amburo. Roberto, who was the other driver for the hotel, saw Captain Jack in the back alley. Roberto knew Captain Jack because he had seen Amburo walk over to the alley and talk with him from time to time. Roberto himself had been wondering where Amburo was. He had covered Amburo's airport runs since that morning when Amburo failed to pick up his first set of guests at the airport after leaving for his morning run. Roberto and Amburo were hired together and had worked the same shifts for years. Yet Roberto knew nothing about Amburo other than that he was, or appeared to be, friends with Captain Jack. Roberto approached Captain Jack asking him if he was there to see Amburo. Captain Jack was hesitant to answer, then replied, "Will I get him in trouble if I say yes?" Roberto answered, "He can't get into any more trouble than he already is." Telling Captain Jack that he did not show up at the airport this morning and adding, "there was no phone call, nothing." This was unlike Amburo and Captain Jack knew it. What the three of them have been doing all these years went unnoticed because they know never to bring attention to themselves and never to misbehave at work, always be professional, and keep a low profile. Anonymity was the key to keeping themselves from getting caught. With Amburo, not showing up, didn't sit right with Captain Jack; he was getting a bad feeling. Captain Jack had questions but knew they were ones Roberto did not have the answers too. He knew he needed to find Amburo. Smiling at Roberto, Captain Jack said "Thank you", then immediately turned and walked away without giving Roberto a chance to say anything or continue the conversation.

An hour later, Captain Jack was back on his boat. He had gone to the jacal where Amburo lived with his mother. There was no sign of him there either. He banged on the door several times very loudly, but no one answered. He was very concerned now and couldn't figure out where Amburo was. Then, in one of those eye-popping moments, a horrible thought hit him. Something was wrong; he never had to knock before; the door was never locked. His mother was the perpetual homebody; she would leave the entry door unlocked even if Amburo wasn't home. Today, he found the entry door locked, the windows closed, and the curtains, drawn. At first, he thought nothing of it. But now he couldn't help but think something was wrong; he just didn't know what. He sat in his Captain's chair behind the wheel of his boat, and staring out at the Caribbean Sea, he wondered if he should just untie the boat and sail down to Paraguay or maybe Bolivia to hide out and start over. His gut was telling him to pack up and run. He needed to put distance between himself and the shanty. He needed to go someplace where no one knew him. After staring out at the sea and pondering this for what seemed like hours, Jeremy made his presence known. Jeremy had boarded the boat with a total disregard for protocol. He boarded without permission. He quietly headed to the bridge of the small vessel and stood in the doorway watching Captain Jack stare at the water. After a few moments, Jeremy raised his hands up to the doorframe and, with open hands, hit the door with quick, sharp slaps like he was playing the bongos, scaring the shit out of Captain Jack..

Chapter 20

Blake arrived at the hotel to pick up Patty for their date using the rear employee entrance instead of the front on this occasion. Blake wasn't a hotel employee, but he did have special privileges and was allowed entrance through the back of the hotel where the employees enter. Blake wanted to check on Mateo, and as he hoped, he ran into him. Mateo was still visibly distraught, even more so than he was earlier. Mateo was at his locker changing into his street clothes when Blake noticed that his street clothes were dusty and dirty as if he had been crawling through sand on the beach. Blake saw that there was a tear running down the side of Mateo's cheek, and he was trembling. While the trembling may have been slight, it was enough to be noticed. Blake knew Mateo and his mother very well. Blake had a soft spot for Mateo because he always felt a certain connection with him that he couldn't explain. For some odd reason, he had a bond with Mateo's mother, too. He felt a kinship with Mateo and couldn't understand why, but Mateo felt like family. It wasn't a motherly bond he felt with Mateo's mother, but he still felt a connection to her he couldn't explain.

Blake never knew his mother, she died when Blake was just a toddler, and his dad was always working, leaving Blake to be raised by a Nanny. Blake tried to comfort Mateo and asked what was wrong, but Mateo refused to answer. He just sat there, silently staring into his locker. Blake tried again, only to receive the same silence from Mateo. Blake was now starting to get an uneasy feeling as Mateo's mother entered the locker room and asked Blake if she could talk to him privately. They went into her small office, and behind closed doors, she told Blake that she was worried sick about Mateo. She told Blake how he didn't come home last night and showed up to work this morning covered in sand. Mateo's mother told Blake she was met with the same response that he received when she tried to talk to him. She went on to tell Blake she didn't know what to do and asked if he would keep trying to get Mateo to tell him what was wrong. She had never seen Mateo like this before, and Blake could see just how worried she was. Blake was quick to agree and told Mateo's mother to take him home, and he would meet them there later.

A few moments later, he was knocking on the door to Patty and Michele's room. He heard Patty say the door was open. He entered the room and saw Patty sitting on the sofa. She was as visibly upset as Mateo. Blake walked over and seated himself next to Patty saying, "Michele hasn't returned yet has she?" Through watery eyes, Patty shook her head. Blake gently put his arms around Patty giving her a supportive hug and allowing her to briefly find some comfort in his arms. He asked Patty when was the last time she saw Michele. After a few sniffles and a deep breath, Patty told Blake that the last time she saw Michele was at the Disco. Without Blake having to ask, Patty told him about Jeremy not showing up for work today and how oddly Mateo was acting too. Blake sat there on the sofa with Patty's head tenderly tucked under his chin, thinking to himself, *what the hell is going on?* Things didn't make sense to Blake. Michele has gone missing, Mateo was clearly upset about something which is not like him, and Jeremy, who never misses work, did not come in today. Blake didn't know why Jeremy wasn't at work today, thinking to himself, *I wouldn't know. I'm a lifeguard hired by the city of Cancun, not a hotel employee.* He remembered seeing Amburo at the Disco and thought he might have seen something. He tried to tell himself that the things going on were just a coincidence; he needed to focus on finding Michele. His gut was telling him otherwise. He knew something wasn't right. He was worried that maybe they had gotten ahold of some bad drugs. The Disco was a well-known spot for dealers. Cutting Cocaine with fentanyl was starting to gain popularity, along with Cocaine becoming the drug of choice. He thought maybe they partied too hard and were in trouble. He was growing concerned and was troubled by the fact that Mateo knew something but was afraid to talk. They both sat in silence for a while, with Blake reassuring Patty that everything would be fine. Blake knew he had to do something. He told Patty that he would go to Jeremy's place to see if they were there. Patty wanted to go, but he told Patty that she should stay there in case Michele returns.

Not knowing where Jeremy lived, Blake went back to Mateo's mother's office to try and catch her before they left, hoping she knew or had access to Jeremy's records to find out where he lived. Mateo and his mother had already left the resort, but luck was on Blake's side. The bartender filling in for Jeremy was just leaving the locker room when Blake arrived. The fill-in bartender wasn't friendly with Jeremy but did know where he lived and was quick to tell Blake. Blake was surprised that he didn't have to come up with a fabricated story as to why he was looking for Jeremy. The fill-in bartender told him where Jeremy lived and continued on his way. Blake hurried to Jeremy's place thinking he was going to find the worst possible scenario. He could not help but think they accidentally overdosed. He was trying to mentally prepare himself, thinking he was going to find two dead bodies. He knew he should have called the Federales to check on them but decided it would be better if he went first. Knowing Mexico and its tough laws and harsh treatment of drug offenders, Blake knew that if the federales found Michele alive and with drugs, she would be arrested on the spot and jailed. There was no bail for drug offenders, and Michele would have to stay in jail until her trial, which would take months. He also knew that she would be facing a lengthy jail sentence if convicted, which was a certainty if caught even with a small amount of drugs. If she were alive, it would be better if he found her and got her out of there. If she were dead, then it didn't matter when he called the Federales. When Blake arrived at Jeremy's, he immediately knocked on the front door. When no one answered, he checked to see if the door was unlocked.

Finding the front door locked, he went to check around back to see if he could see through the windows or if there was a back entrance. He found a back entrance, but that too was locked. He found an open window, which he was able to climb through with ease. Right away, the stench inside caused Blake to wretch, so he stuck his head back out the window, gasping for fresh air. He took a deep breath and held it as he quickly checked the tiny living area and bedroom for them. A scan of the tiny living was all it took before sticking his head out the window again and taking in more fresh air, then holding his breath as he headed into the bedroom. Thankfully, no one was there, and no bodies were found. He was grossed out at how Jeremy lived. It looked like the trash hadn't been taken out in months. The sight of dirty dishes covered in rotting, maggot-infested food that filled the kitchen sink in the tiny kitchenette, caused him to start dry heaving. He turned back to crawl out the same window he entered from, once again gasping for some fresh air. Not finding anyone at Jeremy's was met with both a sigh of relief and frustration. The relief came because he thought the stench might have been coming from their decaying bodies. The frustration was because no one was there, and he didn't know where to look or what to do next. Once he was back out on the street, he realized it was getting later in the evening, and the Disco was opening. He knew that would be the next logical place to check. He could hear the 1970's anthem and disco favorite, "I Will Survive", as he stood outside talking to one of the lifeguards he worked with and who moonlighted as a doorman at the Disco. Palo Rodrigez, who was known by everyone as

Pauly, knew who Jeremy was and despised him. Pauly knew Jeremy was rotten to the core. Jeremy's presence alone made the hair on Pauly's neck stand up. Because of this, he had no issue telling Blake what he wanted to know. He also told Blake to keep him updated on the situation. As Blake turned around to walk away, Pauly grabbed Blake by the upper arm and said in an intimidating tone, "Keeping me updated isn't a request." Letting go of Blake's arm, Pauly stepped back into his position at the entrance to the Disco. Blake was confused by Pauly's loud and aggressive tone. Pauly wasn't, or at least not with Blake, the commanding type. He stared at Pauly for a moment, then started to slowly walk away. Pauly had always been the quiet and polite one: never drawing attention to himself in his personal and professional life. He was a keep-to-himself type of guy. The only one Pauly would talk to and was friendly with was Blake, when he was on lifeguard duty. Pauly kept the conversations between the two superficial, never talking about his personal life with Blake. What Blake didn't know was just who Pauly was and why he kept a low profile, but later that evening, he would find out.

The next stop for Blake was Mateo's house. He had promised Amelia, Mateo's mother, he would be by to talk with Mateo. He arrived at Amelia's la casa de campo, which is what the local Spanish-speaking population called the cottage-style homes on the outskirts of town where Mateo and Amelia were living. Amelia's cottage was very well kept. Gardening was her favorite pastime; the lush grounds were filled with multiple gardens of native plants and flowers. Behind the cottage was a vegetable garden that Amelia took great pride in. The country setting and other small cottages that dotted the sparsely populated area were more a farming community than the lush tropical forest that the Yucatan peninsula was noted for. This is how Blake pictured his future with Patty, whom he was falling in love with even though they had just met. As he walked up to the cottage, he saw Amelia sitting on the small porch waiting for him. Amelia stood up as Blake entered the yard and walked up the small cobblestone path to where she was sitting. Amelia thanked Blake for keeping his promise. She told Blake, "Mateo has agreed to tell you everything on the condition that you, Blake, promise to protect Mateo." Blake asked, "Was he part of whatever is going on?" "No, Mateo hasn't done anything wrong. He was manipulated and Jeremy took advantage him." Blake was intently listening to what Amelia had to say. She continued, "Mateo has diminished cognitive development. Yes, he has the body of a young adult, but his mind is like a child of seven or eight. He didn't know what he was doing. He thought Jeremy was his best work friend." Amelia begged, "Please Blake, promise you will protect him." Blake told Amelia he needed no further explanation or begging; his gut told him he needed to agree and promise to protect Mateo. Without saying another word, Amelia got up off her chair and went inside with Blake following her to the gathering room next to the kitchen where Mateo was sitting and waiting. The gathering room was decorated in typical Mexican tradition with colorfully patterned tiles on the wall and large terracotta tiles on the floor. There was a large hutch-style cabinet on the wall that displayed the festive dinnerware that was only used for special occasions. Mateo was seated at the long wooden farmer's table that was in the center of the gathering room. The table had benches on each side and wooden high-backed chairs with armrests at each end of the table. Blake looked around the room again and thought that this was the home he wanted to raise his children in with Patty. Amelia sat on the bench next to her son and motioned for Blake to take a seat in one of the chairs at the end of the table. Amelia placed a hand on her son's shoulder and told him, "It's Okay Matty, Blake is here to help you and won't let any harm come to you. He will protect us." Matty, is what she called her son. Mateo looked over his shoulder at his mother and with his naive innocence asked, "Will he help the blonde girl with the big boobs too?" Blake answered, saying he promised, then asked if it was the girl from the hotel he was talking about. Mateo was nodding yes as tears slowly rolled down his cheeks again. Blake said, "Tell me everything Matty, I promise I will protect you both." With a trembling jaw, Mateo took a few deep breaths and wiped the tears off his cheeks with the back of his hand, then started to tell Blake everything. He started by telling Blake how he would signal his best friend at work, Jeremy, when pretty girls were traveling alone or if there were girls traveling in a group without their boyfriends. He told Blake, "Jeremy told me about the VIP treatment the hotel gives certain guests, and said he was in charge of taking them to the special VIP spot." Mateo's eyes started filling up again as he told Blake how this time, he got a weird feeling like he needed to watch out for the blonde with the big boobs. Mateo needed to take a few deep breaths before continuing to tell Blake about what happened. Even though he felt safe and trusted Blake, he was still scared. In his neurodivergent mind he was doing the best he could to be brave and do the right thing. Blake patiently waited for Mateo to continue, which he did, wiping the tears off his own cheek with the back of his hand as he spoke. Mateo blushed when he told Blake how he saw Jeremy touch her private parts at the pool bar the first day they were there at the resort. "I didn't like it when he touched her there! He broke the resort's rules! You're not supposed to break the rules." In the manner with which Mateo made that statement, Blake truly saw just how childlike and impressionable he was and realized that Jeremy knew he could easily persuade Mateo into doing anything he needed him to do. Mateo was so impressionable he knew that if Jeremy ever got caught, being the weasel that he is, he would use Mateo as his scapegoat. He knew that Jeremy would say something to the effect that it was Mateo, and he was just trying to stop him. Blake clearly understood why he needed to protect Mateo and why Amelia was so worried. Without any encouragement, Mateo continued telling Blake that on the night that Jeremy took the girl with the big boobs out, he knew he had to follow them. He told Blake that after he saw the girl with the big boobs get into Amburo's car, he jumped on his bicycle and followed them. He told Blake, "I hid watching till they came out again, then I followed them to the sand dunes and saw Jeremy carry her to an abandoned shanty." He told Blake how he crawled under the shanty and watched them through a hole in the floor. He saw how they tied her to the bed and gagged her mouth so she couldn't scream. He watched as a naked Jeremy attacked a naked Amburo after Amburo hit the girl with the big boobs. "I never saw Jeremy that angry before. It scared me." Mateo said he helplessly watched as they all took turns doing "bad things" to her. "When they were done, they left her tied to the bed. I couldn't leave her alone, I needed to stay with her, so I stayed under the shanty all night." Mateo had to stop to collect his thoughts. Blake could see how scared Mateo was and again he vowed to himself to protect Mateo. When Mateo was able to continue, he said he was woken up by Amburo when he returned the next morning. Tears came streaming down Mateo's cheeks as he continued to tell how Amburo assaulted her with the club that policemen carry. He was sobbing when he said her body was lifeless, he thinks she is dead, shouting, "it's my fault she is dead!" Mateo crossed his arms on the table, leaned forward resting his forehead on his crossed arms, and started sobbing, "I'm sorry, it's my fault! I should have stopped them." He said as he started choking on his own spit and whaling "They killed her! She is dead and I just watched and did nothing." Blake grew angry because Mateo kept blaming himself. Knowing Jeremy would have killed Mateo if he found him under the shanty, caused even more internal anger that Blake hid from Mateo and his mother as he tried to calm and soothe Mateo. Amelia put her arms around her son, hugging him tight till he settled down, while both reassured him none of this was his fault.

Finally, after Mateo had settled down somewhat, he went to his bedroom and collapsed on his bed, crying himself to sleep. Blake headed for the front door to leave, with Amelia following him out. Outside, Amelia stopped Blake. More assertive than she was earlier with her plea she begged, "Please promise me nobody will hurt him." Blake looked at her, "I promised you that already, why do you keep asking me to protect him?" Amelia was wringing her hands and staring down at the ground before looking back up at Blake and finding the courage to tell him why. When Amelia didn't answer Blake right away, he said he needed to leave and go find the shanty. Just as he turned to walk away, Amelia blurted out, "Because he is your brother, that's why you need to protect him, because he can't protect himself, he needs his brother." Stunned by what he had just heard, Blake turned around and asked. "My brother?" Amelia told him, "Yes, your half-brother you both have the same father." Amelia quickly explained to Blake that just after he was born, his mother was diagnosed with a cancerous brain tumor. She told Blake that she was the housekeeper for his father and took care of him because his mother was too sick from the chemo treatments. The treatment lasted about two years, but the cancer finally won, His mother passed away just after his second birthday but not before she made her dying wish to her husband. That wish was to let you choose your own path in life and not force you to follow in his footsteps like his father made him do. She told Blake that one night, about six months after his mother's passing, she found his father on the veranda crying. She sat with him to comfort him. It was the first time anyone had seen Blake's father cry. Amelia told Blake, "I was the only one who saw your father's emotions. If he had shown an ounce of vulnerability during the whole ordeal, he would have lost everything. The other Cartel members would have considered him to be weak, no longer able to run the Cartel." Amelia went on to tell Blake how his father would find comfort with her without anyone knowing, which is how he was able to remain as the man in charge. "One-night things went too far; your father and I got caught up in our emotions we slept together. I got pregnant with Mateo. Once I told your father that I was pregnant, he let me go with no explanation." Blake could hear the hurt in her voice. It wasn't hard to figure out that Amelia had fallen in love with him. "He took care of us by buying us this house and giving me a job as head of housekeeping at the resort and giving Mateo a job there when he was old enough to work." She told Blake she knew how ruthless his father was, and if he found out Mateo was involved, he would kill his own son to protect the cartel business. Amelia knew Blake wasn't part of the cartel; his father told her about his wife's dying wish. Blake's father hid his own involvement from Blake, telling him success with the resort was more than he could ever have imagined. Amelia knew that Blake was kept in the dark about the cartel business, but felt he needed to know or he wouldn't be able to protect Mateo. Blake stared at Amelia. He was trying to take it all in. Mateo is his brother, his father is the head of the cartel, and the rumors were true about females being abducted. His mind was trying to process everything. Blake may have been stunned at first by the news he just received, but at the same time he was not surprised and now understood the reason why he has always felt a connection to Mateo. This made him more determined than before to protect Mateo, knowing that he is his younger brother..

Chapter 21

Michele lay tightly bound on top of a moldy mattress trapped inside the old shanty. She was completely helpless and drifting in and out of consciousness, unaware of the assault she suffered earlier in the day. Her subconscious mind was working overtime to protect her from the trauma and abuse she was receiving. It was midday when Michele was semiconscious enough to feel the shooting pain in her groin. The pain she was feeling was intense, bringing tears to her blindfolded eyes. She tried squirming around on the bed in the hope of finding some comfort and relief. The pain was causing her to bite down on her gag so hard that her teeth were tearing through the fabric. Her breathing had become labored, and she was on the verge of a full-blown panic attack. Michele had begun to realize her rapid and shallow breathing, her grunting, and fierce bites on the gag were providing some comfort. The pain she had in her groin was slightly easing. Her breathing was slowly becoming deeper and more controlled as the pressure of her bite helped to relieve her pain with each breath, till the sharp pains dissipated to the point of being tolerable. Even though she had blacked out, her body and mind were both exhausted from the ordeal and from the episode she just had, which had come close to causing a mental crisis that there would be no coming back from. The relief was enough that she was now able to drift off to sleep.

It was early in the evening when Michele woke up. She was able to get some rest even if it were just for a few hours. Outside the air was still and the calm of the Caribbean Sea created a silence on the waters. It was in that stillness, that calm, that eerie silence that allowed Michele to hear the dance music emanating from the Disco; the same Disco she was at just a few nights ago. Michele could hear her favorite song, and in her mind, she was singing parts of the song that stuck out. She sang the parts her subconscious needed her to hear and sing, *No not I, I will survive, I know I'll stay alive, I got my life to live, I will survive, I, I, I will survive!* She was hearing the words she needed to hear and singing the lyrics she needed to sing continuously until it became her mantra. The Mantra she needed to necessitate not only to keep her from a mental breakdown but give her the hope of surviving the ordeal.

The loud rattling of the lock and clasp, followed by the squealing of door hinges in desperate need of lubricant, broke the silence of the night. There were loud footsteps on the wooden floor and mechanical voices that made her captors sound like the robots in the Indie Sci-Fi films Josh loved fill the room. She couldn't tell what the voices were saying; they were keeping their voices low and not directing the conversation to her. She felt two hands gently spread her thighs, exposing her. This time she heard the voices when they said, "Today's cleaning went well I see, fresh and pink and ready for us." "The cleaning crew never disappoints." She didn't know who belonged to the robotic voices or who held her captive, but she knew what was about to happen. She let out a soft moan as she felt something that she was sure was a tongue up against her. The excruciating pain she experienced earlier that day was gone, and she was enjoying what was going on. Whoever was doing this to her was being gentle and giving her pleasure, unlike the previous night. She didn't want it to stop. Performing and receiving oral sex was a form of foreplay Captain Jack loved. He really likes doing it to Michele because he could get her to respond so easily. While Captain Jack was doing his thing, Jeremy warned her not to scream, and he took off her gag and replaced it with the O-ring gag. Michele did let out a loud, "OH GOD" as Captain Jack worked his magic with his tongue. Jeremy smirked when she did that then quickly replaced her gag with the O-ring gag. He noticed the bite marks that tore deep into the cloth rag, not realizing they were from the excruciating pain she suffered earlier, He thought to himself that she must really be enjoying the tongue lashing she was getting from Captain Jack. Jeremy motioned for him and Captain Jack to switch places. Both men shuffled around with Jeremy picking up where Captain Jack left off. Michele knew the guys had switched; the sensation was different but just as pleasurable as the other. Captain Jack was quick to insert himself into Michele's mouth. Michele wanted to spit him out, but because of the gag she knew she couldn't. What was going on between her legs had stopped, and she could hear a scraping noise coming from under the bed. It sounded like something heavy was being dragged across the floor. Seconds later, she could feel her legs being spread open again and something hard being inserted inside her. The moment the hard object was inserted inside her, the same excruciating, sharp pain that she suffered earlier shot through her. She started to scream, but between the O-ring gag and Captain Jack being inside her mouth, she could barely emit an audible gagging sound that went unnoticed by both men. Even though she was blindfolded, the pain was blinding. In her mind's eye, she saw a blinding white light flash before her. When the light had dimmed, the pain was gone, and in her mind, she could see she was surrounded by the crystal-clear waters of the coral reef she had snorkeled in just a few days prior. As she peered deeper into the water, it took on a beautiful hue that reminded her of the aqua marine-colored waters she saw in the brochures back in her hotel room. Vibrantly colored fish started to appear, and a warm sensation came over her. She was no longer afraid; she felt peace and calm overtake her, unlike the last time, when her subconscious heightened her pleasure receptors in her brain as part of "survival mode." This time, Michele had passed out from the pain that was radiating from her pelvic area and was raging through her body. Her subconscious quickly found a recent memory bringing Michele to another place, another time, another realm and reality that she could get lost in, to once again protect her mind and her psyche from the vial and vicious attack on her physical body.

Jeremy was unaware that Michele had passed out from his use of an artificial phallus on her. Jeremy knew nothing of the torture that

Amburo had put Michele through early that day. He did not know the pain he was causing. Michele's body was going limp, startling Captain Jack, rendering him momentarily speechless. He withdrew himself from her mouth, fearing she wasn't breathing. No longer at a loss for words, he gasped, "Hey something's wrong," without the use of his electrolarynx, immediately catching the attention of Jeremy. Jeremy was just about to lose it on Captain Jack for not using the device but as he spoke, he realized Michele's body had become lifeless. "Holy fuck! We killed her!" Jeremy exclaimed as Captain Jack placed two fingers on Michele's neck, checking for a pulse. Jeremy's mind flashed back to when he was standing over Trixie's body this time; he wasn't aroused. The disturbing vision of Trixie lying dead in front of him instead of Michele drove a shivering panic through him. Jeremy's voice quivered as he asked, "Is she dead?" Taking notice of the quiver in Jeremy's voice Captain Jack replied with some relief, "No, I can feel a pulse, she is alive." Jeremy started nervously pacing back and forth as the panic took control. He knew if he got caught, his past would come out. Normally on the receiving end of the orders from Jeremy, Captain Jack took control of the situation. He wasn't so much giving orders as he was trying to calm Jeremy out of his fear that he would be blamed for this. Captain Jack told Jeremy to put the dildo, and whatever else they took out of the old army footlocker, back into the trunk that they stored everything in. Picking his shirt up off the floor, Captain Jack quickly began wiping prints from anything that could produce a fingerprint. Jeremy, seeing what Captain Jack was doing, nervously began doing the same. In their panic, the two men threw on their clothes, but Captain Jack remained shirtless so he could wipe down the exterior of the door and lock. Captain Jack told Jeremy, "Grab the footlocker and anything else that could identify us." Just as Jeremy stepped out the door trying not to drop the footlocker, Captain Jack took one last look, making sure they didn't miss anything. After a quick scan of the room, Captain Jack saw they had left the O-ring gag in her mouth. He quickly picked up the cloth gag and replaced the O-ring gag with it. Jeremy saw Captain Jack going back in, dropping the footlocker as he turned around and barged back into the shanty, yelling, "What the fuck are…" Jeremy stopped himself midsentence when he saw Captain Jack replacing the O-ring gag. Captain Jack stood up and shoved the O-ring gag in his back pocket, telling Jeremy, "Latex could have our fingerprints on it." Jeremy didn't say anything, he silently went back out the door. Captain Jack secured the door to the shanty, then wiped the doorknob and lock. Together both men, grabbed a handle at each end of the footlocker, and made their way through the sand dunes hoping no one would find the shanty or Michele's body till after they were gone and hopefully forgotten. "What are we going to do with this?" Which was more of a demand than a question from Jeremy. Captain Jack told Jeremy he was going to dump the footlocker in the Caribbean Sea several miles offshore, stating no one would ever find it. As the men trekked through the sand dunes, Captain Jack had that uncomfortable feeling he had forgotten something.

Blake left Amelia's house, heading to the sand dunes and the area Mateo had said he followed Amburo to. As he approached the path that led to the sand dunes, he could hear the music from the Disco off in the distance. His mind quickly shifted to when he last saw Michele. It was at the Disco, and she was with Jeremy. He knew the rumors that had been swirling around the rumor mill about certain guests going missing then showing up again a few days later. He brushed them off as just rumors. Just like he brushed off the rumors the resort was owned by the local cartel. But tonight, with the information he was given by his half-brother and Amelia, he got that feeling you get in your gut when you know something is wrong. He started giving credibility to the rumors that he didn't want to believe. Blake didn't want to believe that his father was the head of the cartel. He wanted to believe that his father was a powerful businessman who owned a popular resort in Cancun. He didn't want to believe that women were being raped but now he realizes this was much more than just rumors. The footprints he came across in the loose sand made it easy for him to follow the right path. He was approaching the back of the shanty when he heard Jeremy shout, "Holy fuck! We killed her." Stopping him in his tracks. He stood there frozen in his own footsteps from the stunning words he heard which were followed by Captain Jack saying he found a pulse. Then he heard the commotion of Jeremy and Captain Jack shuffling around. Blake remembered what Mateo told him about there being a hole in the floor that he peered through while watching Amburo earlier that morning. Blake quickly crawled under the shanty to see if he could see what was going on. His view was limited, but he was able to see both men wiping down the bed and getting dressed. Blake lay there silently watching the two until they finally came out of the shanty. Just like Mateo had told him, he crouched down to remain out of view without losing sight of them. He watched them walk off and took note of the direction they were headed. When he felt like they were far enough away, he crawled out from under the shanty and went to the door. He turned the doorknob and tried the door, knowing it would not open. He was testing the lock to see if he could bust it. The door proved to be flimsy at best and without much effort he was able to kick the door open with a few good kicks. Blake saw the battery-operated camping lantern hanging from a hook in the ceiling that Captain Jack unknowingly left behind. Flicking the switch on the lantern, the room filled with a dim light revealing the lifeless body that was bound to the bed and gagged. Blake went over to Michele hoping she still had a pulse and was breathing. Finding a pulse, he knew she needed medical attention and he needed to get her out of there. He worked quickly to free her from her bindings after taking the gag out of her mouth to help her breathe. In the dimly lit shanty, he saw what appeared to be her clothing in the corner. He did his best to get her clothes back on and cover her exposed body. He gently took her in his arms, picked her up off the bed, and headed to the door. He knew she needed medical attention, but he also knew if he involved the local Federales it could cause major problems for his father and his resort. Even his father wasn't immune from the Federales when it came to mistreating the tourists who provided the community with its income. While trying to decide what to do, a figure appeared from behind the shanty. Blake didn't see anyone following him and thought he was alone. The person standing in the shadows behind the shanty had stealthily followed him, waiting just out of sight in the sand dunes till Blake kicked in the door before approaching the shanty while he was inside. Seeing the shadowy figured caused Blake to tense up. He was thinking that Jeremy and Captain Jack heard him bust the door down and they came back. As scared as he was, he demanded whoever it was to show themselves. The shadowy figure identified itself, "It's me Amelia. Is the poor girl alive?" Relieved to hear her voice, Blake replied to Amelia, "Yes, but she desperately needs medical attention." Amelia, using a commanding voice told Blake, "Do not go to the hospital take her to my place. My sister is a nurse, she will help her." Amelia continued, "If you take her to the hospital, the Federales will be notified. They will ask questions that you will not want to answer. Let your father deal with the bastards who did this to her." Blake was reluctant to agree, but Michele needed immediate medical attention and he knew she was right; his father would handle this, and the ones who did this would pay dearly. Blake knew they needed to leave now and quickly get her to Amelia's sister, so arguing with her would only worsen Michele's condition. Blake did not see the three indistinguishable figures standing and watching them from the top of the sand dunes as they swiftly navigated their way through and back to the street. Amelia was making sure they stayed in the shadows and out of the public eye once they were out of the sand dunes and in the streets that lead back to Amelia's. Blake thought to himself, *for a woman in her fifties she moved with the grace of a gazelle.*

Chapter 22

Amelia came to a stop in the road a short distance from their destination. She told a winded Blake, who was breathless and gasping for air wondering to himself, *how the hell did she come all this way and not be out of breath,* to keep going and take her in through the back entrance and remain out of sight. She instructed him to take her into the gathering room and lay her on the sofa and that she would be along momentarily. Amelia darted off into darkness to get her sister to give Michele the medical attention she needed. Amelia kept praying that Michele didn't need the Emergency room. Blake did as instructed, by bringing Michele through the back and into the gathering room. Just as he was laying Michele on the sofa, Amelia came in with her sister Sophia carrying a medical bag. In a flash, Sophia jumped into action examining Michele. She told Blake to go and bring her a pitcher of water and wash cloths, adding not to return until he was called back into the room. Without question, Blake obliged and hastily headed to the linen storage and bathroom to get the supplies. Sophia didn't want Blake to see her perform a rape examination on Michele. Both Amelia and Sophia removed what little clothing Michele had on and positioned her so Sophia could perform her exam. The bruising on her inner thighs was not as severe as the pelvic and vaginal bruising. She also noticed there was the appearance of tearing and slight bleeding coming from within Michele's vagina. Using her diagnostic pen light from her medical bag and gloved hands Sophia spread Michele's labia majora open giving her a better view so that she could assess the trauma to the area. Although Michele suffered severe trauma to that area at the hands of Amburo, the injuries appeared to be minor and required no surgical intervention or medical treatment other than the few sutures that Sophia could do there. Covering Michele back up, Sophia called Blake to bring her the pitcher of water and wash cloths. Blake set the items down next to Sophia as Amelia motioned for Blake to join her in the other room while Sophia cleaned up Michele.

Blake stood in the kitchen with his back to Amelia staring out the window looking into the night as if he were searching for an answer on what to do next. Amelia stood in the center of the room, her hands clasped together with her elbows bent and her head bowed as if she was praying, finally broke the silence, "Is what they did as horrible as Mateo described?" Blake was silent as he tried to find the right words and contain his rage. After a few moments, he replied with a somber, "Yes." followed by a heavy sigh. Amelia knew Blake was processing an overwhelming amount of information he had received that evening: finding out who his father really was, Mateo being his half-brother and what he had witnessed at the shanty. She also sensed he was struggling to process it all. She asked Blake, "Mateo was right, wasn't he? Jeremy did this to her didn't he?" It was a hard question for her to ask, but a question that needed to be asked. Blake stood silent, not wanting to answer. His silence was all Amelia needed to hear. His silence told her that he knew it was Jeremy in the shanty. She approached Blake knowing he didn't know what to do next. Amelia slid her arm between Blake's arm and side, clasping her hands together and resting her head on his shoulder, trying to provide some comfort and support. Once again, silence filled the room, but this time the silence was broken with Sophia entering the kitchen to give them an update on Michele's condition. "Michele is battered and bruised. There was some vaginal tearing from the abuse but otherwise she seems physically ok." Blake stood staring out the window as Sophia continued, "Mentally is another story. She is going to need professional care for the emotional trauma." Sophia finished by telling them she would know more in the morning as she is resting comfortably now. Sophia said she gave Michele a mild sedative to help her sleep and would monitor her condition through the night. Amelia released her hands and turned so she and Blake were facing each other. Amelia took each of Blake's hands into her own. Now face to face, she told him to go and find Pauly, he will know what to do next. Blake, confused, looked at Amelia. Amelia didn't need to be a mind reader because she could easily tell by Blake's facial expression what she needed to say. Amelia told Blake he could trust Pauly and tell him everything. "Do as he says, you can trust him. He will help you." Sarcastically Blake replied, "Let me guess another brother I don't know about?" Amelia lowered her head not out of guilt for hiding the truth from him but out of understanding and compassion. Amelia knew this was all too much for a young man of nineteen to deal with. Amelia looked back up at Blake and softly lied, "No, he isn't but he is someone you can trust like one." Amelia hugged Blake then released him telling him to go before it became too late to find them. Amelia knew it wasn't the time for Blake to find out that on top of everything else his father was a womanizer.

Chapter 22

As the dreary dawn broke, shedding its gloomy light across the everglades on All Hallows Eve, three dark figures peered through the tall sawgrass of the swap at the red 1987 Pontiac Fiero and its female driver. Void of the bright Florida's rising sun, there was an unusually sullen and eerie quiet emanating from the overcast sky of the swamp. The building pressure from the female driver's bladder was causing her to stir and slowly wake from a night of uninhibited sleep. A sleep that was free of the harsh night terrors that normally would take hold of her every night. Still groggy, she incoherently opened the car door and stepped to the rear of the car. Her mind disconnected from the reality around her as she leaned against the rear of the car in a squatting position and began to urinate, unaware that she had not slid her clothing down. Moments later, standing in her urine-soaked clothing, she opened the driver's door and reached in to retrieve the gun she dropped before re-entering the car. Once again, seated behind the wheel of her car with her eyes closed, she raised the gun to the side of her head trying to pull the now frozen trigger. She tried repeatedly to pull the frozen trigger till her arm grew tired and fell limp, dropping the gun onto the floor of that car. Her head fell forward onto the steering wheel. She slumped and slid to the left with her head coming to a rest on the side window once again unconscious and oblivious to her actions.

Chapter 23

Blake left Amelia's and headed straight for the Disco. He didn't want to involve Pauly because he wasn't sure who Pauly was or if he could even trust him. Being the intimidating doorman, he was, in addition to his size, made Pauly a good back up man for Blake. Knowing he wasn't going to be able to confront Captain Jack and Jeremy alone was the only reason he agreed to take Pauly with him. Blake didn't think he needed to tell Pauly what they did to Michele or how he found out. Mentioning the rumors of this happening to other women now had some serious credibility and he wondered if Pauly was involved too. He wasn't even sure if he could trust Amelia in this either even though his gut told him otherwise. She seemed to know how to handle Michele but remained quiet about how she knew. He learned to trust his instincts and if he had a gut feeling that he should go with it. After all, that's what made him the only lifeguard with a perfect save record. Tourists were not noted for obeying or listening to warnings about strong undertows or rip tides. Whenever there was a tropical disturbance in the Caribbean Sea or even a little further north in the Gulf of Mexico, dangerous under currents in the waters would be present. Blake seemed to always know which of the beach goers would get caught up in those under currents or where to look for them if they got pulled out too far. That gut feeling he always led him in the right direction before it was too late. He quickly learned to trust that feeling, that same feeling he was experiencing now, that gut feeling that he knew he could trust Amelia. He decided that if she said Pauly would know what to do, then he should trust that he would.

Pauly was in the same spot he was earlier that night when Blake approached the Disco. Even though Pauly had no updates for Blake, he wasn't surprised to see Blake again that night. Although Jeremy was the most frequent and popular local lounge lizard, who never missed a night at the Disco, he was nowhere to be seen this evening. This led Pauly to believe there was a major problem. Pauly thought to himself, *maybe that little asshole finally overdosed*. With the amount of coke Jeremy was known to snort, overdosing was a logical conclusion. As Blake got closer, he quickly sensed that wasn't it and Blake was going to need his help. The look on Blake's face was all he needed to see to come to that conclusion. As Blake approached, Pauly walked toward him and told Blake, "Let's go to wherever it is you need to take me and fill me in on the way." For some reason Blake wasn't surprised that Pauly knew something wasn't right. Blake quickly led Pauly to the path at the edge of the sand dunes. He had filled Pauly in as much as he could by the time they arrived at the edge of the sand dunes. Blake didn't want to, but he instinctively filled Pauly in on most everything. He did leave out the part of Mateo, being the one who told him about the shanty and that they were half-brothers. Unbeknownst to Blake, Pauly already knew the three of them were brothers. There were many things Pauly knew about Blake and the goings on with the resort and Blake's father's business. Blake did not know Pauly was his father's right-hand man and that Pauly was next in line to run the cartel. His father kept his promise to Blake's mother and honored her dying wish. Instead of bringing Blake up through the ranks, Blake's father brought his third son Pauly up through the ranks. He was his first son that he had before marrying Blake's mother. Blake was never told about his half-brothers because his mother didn't want him to know what she had only found out on her death bed. This is when his father confessed to Blake's mother who he actually was. Hearing this she made him make the promise to never tell who he was and not to let Blake become what he had become.

When they arrived at the edge of the sand dunes Blake stopped walking and turned to look at Pauly asking him, "Just who the hell are you? I know you are not just a doorman." Pauly cracked a half-assed smile and replied, "Dude I am just a part time doorman at the Disco and full-time lifeguard by day." Blake knew better and asked him, "If you are just a doorman and lifeguard, why did Amelia insist I come to you?" Before Pauly could say anything, Blake added that she told him he would know what to do. Pauly knew he wasn't going to be able to maintain the doorman cover with Blake. Because of that Pauly came right out and told Blake he worked for his father. He told Blake his father had caught wind of the rumors of women going missing then turning up again a few days later refusing to talk or go to the Federales.

Pauly told Blake that his father began to suspect Jeremy was involved. When Jeremy first arrived in Cancun, the Federales, along with a Texas Ranger who was on the Cartel payroll, came looking for Jeremy. At the time, the Texas Rangers did not have a current picture of Jeremy, they only had the one picture Trixie had when she took Jeremy in, which they found in Trixie's trailer. Jeremy had altered his look when he first crossed the Texas border into Mexico and flew under the radar, avoiding drawing attention to himself and it seemed to work. The fake ID and credentials even looked real enough to be authentic. There were several employees who were on the Cartel's payroll that were employed by Mexico's version of the IRS, the Servicio de Administración Tributaria. Being a large donor to certain political figures had its perks. The Cartel had certain employees at the Servicio de Administración Tributaria who oversaw the reporting of the resort's employees' payroll. They would turn over the records from the resort for "special" processing. Working for the resort and not having his payroll reported helped Jeremy stay well hidden in plain sight. Shortly after Jeremy started working at the resort, every so often a young female guest would go missing for a few days and suddenly be found at the airport waiting for an early flight back home or she would stay in her room till her stay had concluded. Not one of the women would talk about where they were or what happened. It wasn't long after that Jeremy was able to seek out Captain Jack and Amburo. It was as if each could sense one another and know what one another was thinking. They felt a certain kinship even though they were not related in any sense of the word and they were from different parts of the world. Once Jeremy felt confident he was safe, and no one would ever find out his past, he started using the resort and the Disco as his place to abduct the women with the aid of Captain Jack and Amburo. He would manipulate Mateo and use Mateo as a scout to help him choose his victims wisely. Blake's father always had an uneasy feeling when it came to Jeremy and there was something familiar about him. He didn't realize it was a much older and slightly altered version of the young prepubescent boy, of maybe twelve, in the picture he was shown. Blake's father, (from whom Blake gets his intuition) had a gut feeling about Jeremy. He sent Pauly to start snooping around. Pauly could tell Blake had heard enough for one night when Blake shook his head, not so much in disbelief, but in an information overload kind of way. When Pauly had finished, Blake just turned and headed into the sand dunes to show Pauly the shanty and the direction the two men went. Pauly wanted to tell his brother who he really was, but knew it wasn't his call to make. One thing he did learn from his father was never to cross him. The cartel had a way of dealing with those who didn't follow orders. Even his own son wasn't immune to his father's wrath.

Blake kept his head up acting like a lookout while Pauly kept his head low following the tracks. The tracks in the sand were easy to follow. Neither Jeremy nor Captain Jack tried or even thought about covering their tracks, which led Blake and Pauly right to the pier where Captain Jack docked his boat. Their carelessness also led to Captain Jack dropping the O-ring gag in the sand dunes. Pauly saw the O-ring gag and picked it up showing Blake what he found in the sand saying,

"They certainly came this way." Blake recognized the O-ring gag right away and knew Pauly was right. They reached the pier and noticed there was just one boat that had light coming from the port hole. The other boats were dark; Blake quickly recognized the boat with the lights on as Captain Jack's. Pauly silently led the way down the pier. Both he and Blake did their best ninja impersonation as they tactically made their way towards Captain Jack's boat. Pauly put a finger to his lips to signal Blake to be quiet as they kept out of sight. When they were about ten feet or so from the boat, Pauly motioned for Blake to stay put as he got down on his belly and slithered forward to get a better view of who was on the boat. He found both men in the front cabin just below the front deck. Jeremy and Captain Jack were trying to figure out what to do about Michele and how they could pin everything on Amburo and Mateo. They were seated at the galley table. Not only was it Captain Jack's tour boat, but it was also where he called home. The front cabin had a tiny galley kitchen and seating area that served as both a dining area and living room. There was a small hallway the led to the bunk area and bathroom fit for a single occupant. Both Captain Jack and Jeremy were making plans to dump the chest they hauled back to the boat. They were also discussing retrieving Michele and dumping her with the chest after they torched the shanty. They both knew if they turned on Amburo and tried to pin everything on him and Mateo, he would take them down with him. Their best option was to destroy all the evidence and leave Cancun for Argentina, where they knew they could easily hide out.

Pauly continued casing the boat. He saw they had left the gang plank in place giving him and Blake easy access to the boat. Pauly, still on his belly, slithered his way back to Blake and told him what he saw. Pauly quickly came up with a plan for he and Blake to lure the men to the top deck so they could capture and subdue them. This time Pauly didn't get down on his belly as he and Blake quickly made their way to the boat that housed both Jeremy and Captain Jack. Being that there was no view of the gang plank from the porthole, Pauly knew that they could board without being detected. Pauly was able to sneak aboard and hide from sight. After Pauly was out of sight Blake boarded the boat and stood towards the stern facing the door. Once he was in position and got the nod from Pauly, Blake shouted, "Hey Jack why don't you and that tiny-dicked friend of yours come up on deck, we need to talk." Being called tiny-dicked would always trigger Jeremy's uncontrollable rage. This time was no different. Jeremy bolted up from the galley table and ran for the stairs that took him from below to the top deck with Captain Jack right behind him. Jeremy burst through the door to find Blake standing on the deck holding up the O-ring gag. Jeremy stopped dead in his tracks. He instantly went from rage to panic. Captain Jack stopped behind Jeremy, who was blocking the door but was able to see what Jeremy was seeing, causing enough fear to paralyze him where he stood. "Drop something?" Blake asked. Jeremy trying to get his wits about him angrily replied, "You little fuck give that to me!" "Come and get it." Blake told him. Jeremy hated it when anyone talked back to him. Now with a mix of panic and rage Jeremy tried to lunge forward and attack Blake. With lightning speed, a closed fist came out of nowhere, catching Jeremy in the jaw and knocking him flat on his back. Jeremy lay there staring up at the stars before blacking out. With catlike reflexes Pauly quickly turned and with a side kick he sent Captain Jack tumbling down the stairs to the lower deck. Blake quickly rolled Jeremy over onto his stomach, and hog tied him with the rope they found on the pier. Pauly barreled through the open door ascending the stairs and hog-tying Captain Jack. Pauly took a couple of rags he managed to find on the boat and used them as a -gag while Blake used the O-ring gag on Jeremy. With the two men gagged, they were unable to yell for help. Pauly locked Captain Jack below deck in the engine compartment which was nothing more than a crawl space then headed top side to where Blake was watching guard over Jeremy. Jeremy was still out of it from the blow he took from Pauly's fist, making it easy for Blake and Pauly to tie him to the pole they managed to find. They used the pole to carry Jeremy, like a hunter does with their prize kill, back to the shanty.

Chapter 24

Hours later, with the dank overcast sky still looming, the female driver awoke to the putrid smell of her own urine and the uncomfortable feeling of wet clothing. She had no recollection of what happened just a few hours ago. Sitting back in the upright position, flashbacks of the recent past came flooding back into her mind. The past she could no longer outrun; the past that no matter the amount of cocaine or alcohol she consumed, it was a past that could not be erased from her mind. Unable to handle the barrage of the vivid and horrid memories being replayed in her mind, she instinctively reached for the bottle of vodka that was in her bag on the passenger seat. Her hands were shaking so badly she was barely able to unscrew the cap and needed to steady the bottle with both hands so she could raise the bottle to her mouth without dropping it. She began guzzling the clear fluid, tolerating the burning in her throat from the fiery liquid till she couldn't tolerate it anymore. She managed to consume a large amount of the vodka before her choking caused her to spew the mouthful of goriachee vino onto the windshield. The ill effects of alcohol were almost instantaneous. Her empty stomach provided an immediate pathway to her blood stream. She barely had enough time to recap the bottle before passing out again under the dreary early afternoon skies, shrouded in the dismal gloom of the soundless swamp.

A moment later the three dark figures watching her slowly drifted back into the tall saw grass.

Chapter 25

Blake and Pauly managed to get Jeremy into the shanty. Pauly told Blake, "Drop him on the floor, even that bed is too good for him." Blake was happy to oblige and dropped Jeremy onto the floor. Jeremy let out a groan as his body thudded on the hard surface. Pauly told Blake, "I will take it from here," insisting it was time for him to go. Blake wasn't going anywhere and demanded, "I am going to see this through to the end." Blake insisted on getting the Federales involved to arrest both of Michele's rapists. He also tried to stand firm about taking Michele to a hospital, telling Pauly she needed more than just the first aid that Amelia's sister provided. Pauly grabbed Blake by the shoulder and squeezed hard enough to cause Blake to bend at the knees. Pauly firmly held him in place, and in a commanding voice said, "I got this." Then he leaned in and in the same tone said, "There will be no calls to Federales and no hospitals. I will take it from here." Blake tried to speak but Pauly didn't give him the chance, "Amelia told you I would know what to do. So, trust me, I got this, it will be handled." He assured Blake that Amelia's sister would have taken Michele to the hospital if she needed it. "She didn't, so let her take care of Michele." Blake knew he shouldn't push it any further. Pauly told Blake to go back and check on Michele and see that she is in good hands, if he needed reassurance. He also told Blake he needs to head back to the resort because that brunette he was with the other night came looking for him earlier that night.

Earlier that evening Patty got tired of waiting around for Blake to show up. Feeling like she had been stood up she headed out to see if she could find Michele. Knowing the Federales would be no help and knowing what trouble Michele could get into because of the pot she had hidden in her luggage, Patty decided to head out on her own. Bravely she walked several back streets in hopes of maybe finding her best friend. She knew those back streets were going to be seedy. She also knew those back streets held unknown dangers for tourist especially young females. Patty held the fear that the person she grew up with, the person she idolized and wanted to be like, the one person from the small town in Maine where they were born and raised and that she truly cherished, could be lying dead in an alley. Patty couldn't live with herself if she didn't try to do something to find Michele. As frightened as she was, Patty mustered up the courage to venture out risking her own safety and possibly her life to find Michele. As Patty walked down the dark streets, her nostrils quickly filled with stench of stale urine and decaying garbage. Not knowing if the stench that turned her stomach was human or animal caused her to dry heave and even spit up some of the liquid contents of her stomach. The back streets were dimly lit, and most of the alleys were darker than the streets, but she continued her search regardless of how scared she was or how bad the stench was. It was the thought of going home alone and having to tell Michele's parents she had no idea where Michele was that was driving Patty on. Patty peered down one of the alley ways. Something had caught her attention, but she was unsure of what it was in the dark alley that had her attention. Patty was hesitant to enter the alley way, but she knew if Michele was down there, she had no choice but to go and find her. The alley was fifty feet long and dead ended into a building with a rusty old steel door and a flickering light above. Nervously, she started down the alley. There was a dumpster halfway down the alley along with a stack of empty pallets. Patty reached the dumpster and was quickly overcome with a strong pungent nauseating odor. The odor immediately triggered the memory of the rotting deer carcass she stumbled upon in the woods. The deer was crossing the road one night near the dirt bike trails that she liked to go hiking on and forage for wild blueberries, when the deer was struck by a logging truck. The deer was thrown from the road and into the woods by the overloaded, speeding logging truck. Old Emmit Wilson wasn't much for rules of the road, he liked to run his truck late at night to avoid the law. The old Peterbilt with the steel brush guard that protected the truck from any real damage just kept going, leaving the deer to rot. The dog days of August came early in the summer of 1978. The then eleven-year-old Patty Simons was walking the dirt bike trails on her way to her favorite blueberry picking spot when she smelled the rank stench of the rotting corpse. Being a curious child, she needed to find out what was causing the odor that nearly caused her to vomit up her breakfast. In her search, Patty tripped over the well-hidden rotting carcass falling right into a slimy pool of liquid, that once was the internal organs of the animal. From the time the deer was hit by Emmit's truck to the moment Patty fell into the rotting organs, it had been relentlessly hot and humid causing the rotting carcass to wreak to the high heavens, as her mother would say. The slime covered the entire front of Patty. When Patty got home her mother made her strip down to her underwear before allowing her into the house. The odor that was emanating from Patty's clothes was the most grotesque thing Patty's mother ever smelled. She had to throw the clothing in the trash because no matter how many times she tried, she couldn't get the putrid smell to wash out of her daughter's clothing. Patty was afraid to look in the dumpster. She kept thinking her worst fear had come true, and it was Michele's decomposing body she was smelling. Patty started crying and wanted to get as far away from that dumpster as she could. but she knew she had to look. She crept over to the steel container and peered in. Beneath the flies and maggots that were feasting away on what was at the bottom of the container, and to her relief Patty could see the remnants of what used to be chickens. She couldn't tell how many were in the dumpster but could see there were several rotting carcasses. Still gagging from both the site and smell of the rotting chickens, Patty took a few steps back from the dumpster and now had a clear view of the rest of the empty alley. The flickering light above the steel door stopped flickering long enough and provided enough light for Patty to see the only thing in that alley was remnants of a cock fight which explain the contents of the dumpster and the few rats trying to scrounge up a free meal. She quickly made her way back to the street and continued her search.

Patty continued down the street surrounded by the run-down buildings that were home to Cancun's criminal low life, addicts, and prostitutes. The culture shock was extremely overwhelming to the naive small-town girl from the woods of Maine. Patty experienced the most when it came to the slums was the public housing project of Kennedy Park and the Munjoy Hill Section on the East end of Portland Maine. Her mother and members of her church went to that area to spread the word of the good book and find lost souls they could convert to their cult like church. What she saw in Cancun was far worse than anything she saw in Kennedy Park. In this slum she saw vagrants pushing their shopping carts, with their entire lives packed into them, down the alley ways trying to find a spot to sleep for the night or a dumpster that may have their next meal in it. There were alcoholics sleeping off their latest bender in their tiny homes that had the Frigidaire or Maytag logo on the side. There was a woman passed out with her panties around her ankles and her mini skirt lifted slightly above hips with a needle sticking out of her arm and a rubber band tied just above the elbow to expose the vein. Patty silently prayed that she didn't find Michele here in that condition.

Patty came across a house at the edge of the slum with no lights on. It was the only house or building that was shrouded in complete darkness. She felt as if the house was calling to her yet telling her to stay away at the same time, sending an eerie shiver down her spine. Patty had a major case of the heebie jeebies that kept her frozen in her tracks. In that confusion of that mixed mental message, she felt in her mind she had to check the house out for the sake of her best friend. Patty also needed peace of mind that if the outcome of her search was her worst fear coming true, at the very least she knew she faced her fears and tried to find her friend. She thought, *how could I live with myself if I didn't try looking here and she dies here because I was too afraid to look.* Knowing this, she faced her fears and tried to find her best friend. Searching would, at the very least, provide some solace for her. With that, Patty started towards the house. As she got closer to the house, she noticed the mailbox out front was full and was overflowing. This was unlike the postal service in her hometown who would call for a welfare check if this happened, like the time Old Mrs. Wilson fell and broke her hip. It was the mail delivery man who called for a welfare check. If it wasn't for that call, Old Mrs. Wilson would not have been found for days because her son was on a hunting trip. The Correos de México, the postal service in Mexico, just kept stuffing mail into the box. Walking past the mailbox and up the small walkway to the front of the house Patty could feel the presence of death if self. Even though it was summer in Cancun, Patty could feel the air around her getting colder the further she stepped past the mailbox and onto the property. Patty walked around the house trying to find a window to see inside; she was now deep into the property and feeling that bone chilling cold you get on a raw stormy night in late November. Patty had goose bumps on her exposed skin and she was starting to shiver, making her forget the summer mugginess of the subtropical evening. It felt as if there was a presence trying to push her away from the house: trying to tell her she didn't belong there, there was nothing there for her to see. It was like she heard a voice in her head demanding she leave immediately. It sounded like the voice was telling her Michele wasn't there. Patty refused to let any of that deter her and continued to search for an open door or window to enter through so she could see for herself if her friend was there or not. Patty had worked her way to the back of the house where she saw a set of steps that led to a small stoop and rear entrance. Unknown to Patty, there was a black cat lying at the front of the steps. She managed to step over the cat as she climbed the stairs to see if the door was open and gain access to the interior of the house. She wiggled the door handle several times hoping that maybe she could force the doorknob to turn. Finally, realizing that she wasn't getting in through that door, she started back down the steps to try the other side of the house. The black cat had its eyes fixated on the rodent that was feasting on the moldy remnants of an evening meal partially consumed then discarded several days ago by the occupants of the house. Neither one was aware of the other as Patty started to ascend the step of the small stoop that led her to the back door. Patty stepped off the last step, landing on the black cat's tail and causing the cat to let out a terrifying screech. The sudden screeching from the cat caused every bit of pent-up anxiety that had been building up inside Patty since Michele's disappearance to spew out of her like a volcano's explosive eruption spewing lava and ash miles high into the sky. Her own fear-laden shrieking drowned out the black cat's screeching causing the cat to bolt off in one direction, and Patty in the direction she came from. Patty stopped running when she reached the middle of the street in front of the dark house. She was doubled over with her chest heaving trying to regain her breath. Her heart was racing from the physical exertion and sudden shock from the scare the cat gave her. In the backyard, the mouse sat in the corner enjoying the dinner show, then headed towards the house once the yard was free of its predator. Finding a crack in the wall that was just large enough for it to slip through, the mouse went on searching for another meal. Once Patty had calmed down, she stood in the street in front of the dark house realizing every window she tried to look in not only gave a stronger feeling that death itself was present, it also filled her nostrils with a wretched stench that sent her olfactory nerves haywire. It was a smell she had never experienced before. She thought that this what the smell of death itself would smell like, thinking it was the smell of the Grimm Reaper coming to collect the souls of those whose time on earth had ended. The feeling of not belonging there grew stronger, along with the gut feeling of knowing Michele wasn't there. Even though Patty was unaware of the grizzly scene inside the house, which would become the mouse's next meal, Patty knew death was there. Not knowing how, she just knew it was time to walk away and look for Michele someplace else.

Patty, not knowing where else she could search or what else she could do to find her best friend, headed back to the resort. When she arrived back, the first thing she did was check their room to see if Michele had returned. Before slipping the key into the lock and opening the door to the room, Patty squeezed her eyes shut and tried wishing Michele back safe and sound and that this whole thing never happened. After a moment Patty twisted the key, unlocked the door and stepped into an empty room with no sign of Michele's return. Patty couldn't stand not finding Michele, and the thought of never seeing her again was too overwhelming-- staying in that empty room for a moment longer was too much to handle. She needed to get out of there and go find some place quiet to think. She headed out to the beach and walked to Blake's lifeguard shack. Patty reached the shack and sat down in the sand on the front side of the lifeguard shack facing the Caribbean Sea. She sat with her knees bent and her arms wrapped around her legs. Patty rested her forehead on top of her knees and started sobbing.

Blake started to leave, but not before Pauly told him, "Not a word of this to anyone, not even the brunette." Blake despised the fact that Pauly was right; he could feel it in his gut, but it didn't help with his feelings of guilt knowing he had to lie to Patty. He knew Michele was in good hands and received more than just first aid. He also knew it was best to say nothing to anyone no matter what, especially Patty. That was the part he really hated, having to lie to Patty, the girl he fell in love with on their first date. When he left the shanty, he headed to the resort via the beach versus the city streets. Staying out of sight was best. He needed time to process the overabundance of information that weighed heavily on his young mind. The solitude of the deserted beach gave him some time to do that. He quickly navigated through the sand dunes and passed the pier where Captain Jack was still tied up in his boat. Blake didn't look up or slow down; he just kept his eyes forward and walked with a purpose down the beach. Blake's mind was trying to sort through all the information that was dumped on him that evening. He always knew his legal name was Bakarne Jaun Diaz, his mother Americanized his name to Blake Jon Davis. He knew the reason, or was at least told by his father, that his mother wanted him to be able to cross the border to attend university in the states and start a life there. His father would tell Blake she only wanted what was best for him and leave it at that. He didn't know she wanted him to have a life far from the cartels and wanted him to live in the country she was from. Blake's mother didn't think it was a mistake to marry his father; she truly loved her husband even though he was part of the Cartel. She did want a better life for her son, a life far from the Cartel. Blake's father honored his dying wife's wishes and kept Blake far from the Cartel business. The night air was still, and the Caribbean Sea was calm as he walked along the beach. There was nothing to distract his thoughts as he continued his trek towards the resort. Blake reached the resort and headed straight for Patty's room. The pool area was empty as he passed through and entered the corridor that led to her room. He knocked on the door a few times and when Patty didn't answer he told the empty room he was sorry and he didn't stand her up. He said to her he had a family issue to deal with. He asked the empty room to please understand and open the door. The room remained silent, and the door unanswered. Blake didn't blame

Patty for not answering the door, hoping she didn't feel like she had been stood up by him. Just as he was leaving, that feeling he got in his gut returned, telling him to go back to the beach. He walked out onto the beach and decided to head over to the lifeguard shack. Blake knew he could get a better view of the beach if he stood on the lookout deck of the shack. When he got to the shack, he found Patty sitting in the sand rocking back and forth crying. She was sitting on the opposite side of where he came from which kept her hidden from view. Blake was relieved to find her here and felt a bit foolish at the same time knowing he had pleaded to her through a locked door and an empty room. Without saying a word, he sat behind Patty with his legs apart so he could pull her close to him. Patty scooted sideways so she could rest her head on his chest. Blake wrapped his arms around Patty, pulling her close to him, telling her, "It will be okay, I promise." Patty asked how he knew everything would be ok. Blake told Patty, "I wouldn't lie to the person I am in love with." Blake took a deep breath and said, "I love Patty." Patty snuggled up to Blake whimpering and sniffling before replying, "I love you too Josh.

Chapter 26

Sophia was sitting at the table in the gathering room, keeping a watch over Michele. From where she was seated at the table, she could easily monitor Michele. Amelia had gone to lay on her bed and get some rest. Exhaustion from the events that happened that evening had set in. Michele had been awake for about thirty minutes; the sedative Sophia had given her was mild and did not take long to wear off. She wasn't sure where she was, but she knew she was no longer tied up in the shanty. Michele didn't know if she was safe and was reluctant to let her current captors know she was awake just yet. Michele was trying to take in her surroundings and saw she was in someone's home. The house was small but clean and orderly. Unlike the shanty, there was no foul odor. Michele didn't know who or if anyone was in the room until Sophia spoke. Having a good view from where she was sitting, Sophia saw that Michele had opened her eyes and was awake. Michele heard a soft voice tell her she was safe now, that no one was going to hurt her. Michele didn't believe her but did find the soft tone and calmness in her voice reassuring though she wasn't convinced she was safe. Michele remained silent when Sophia called out; she stayed motionless on the sofa, too scared to get up. Sophia said nothing else, she just let Michele be and went back to stitching the quilt she was making. A labor of love the patchwork quilt represented all the women she had cared for over the years. They were mostly victims of sex crimes or young girls who were trafficked by sexual predators. Tonight, she was creating a patch that resembled a beach shanty which was her way of adding Michele to the quilt. Sophia shed a tear over each patch she had created, with tonight being no different. With every tragic patch she made was also the comfort and solace of knowing those were the lives she saved. The girls and women that she helped heal, both physically and mentally from the cruel and savage world of sex trafficking were memorialized in her quilt. She did have the help of Amelia who would help relocate the victims to safe areas and helped the women find jobs through the resorts network. Although the resort was owned by Blake's father, the resort itself was part of a franchise and international vacation network. Because of this, Sophia also had the protection of the Cartel. Blake's father did have one redeeming quality, and that was the protection and resources he provided to both Amelia and Sophia to help these victims. Sexual predators and pedophiles were people he loathed. He had met his wife, Blake's mother because she was one of the victims Sophia had rescued. It was love at first sight, and after learning her story, he made sure Sophia had all the protection and resources needed. This was why Amelia insisted Blake let his father and Pauly handle Jeremy and anyone else that was involved.

Michele had fallen back to sleep. Although the sedative had worn off, the groggy effects did linger. She had only slept for an hour when the rising pressure in her bladder woke her. Sophia knew Michele was most likely dehydrated from her ordeal. She wasn't wrong, Michele was suffering from mild dehydration which the intravenous fluid resolved quickly. Sophia had administered the intravenous fluid when she first arrived to treat Michele. Michele took a moment before sitting up and trying to get a sense of where her body hurt. She felt pain all over her body with the most intense pain radiating from her midsection and between her legs. Taking a deep breath to help with any discomfort, she slowly started to get herself into a seated and upright position. She was surprised at how little effort it took considering the way her body ached. Once she was upright, she looked around the room trying to locate the person who owned the voice she heard earlier. Before she spotted where Sophia was, Michele heard Sophia say, "Bathroom is just down the hall, here let me help you up." Michele quickly snapped back, "I don't need your help leave me alone!" Experience told Sophia Michele was scared and disoriented and knew not to insist on helping her up or to react to her anger-filled response. Her experience taught her that it was best to wait for her to ask for help. The aches in her body were mild in comparison to the way her head felt. Michele's head was throbbing with a fierce pain that she had never felt before. This was a side effect from the drugs her captures had used on her to keep her sedated while they were gone. The pain in her head was debilitating but she did manage to scoot herself to the edge of the sofa. She saw her purse and shoes on a small coffee table in front of the sofa. She was still wearing the clothing from the night she went missing. Her bra and panties were not with her clothes when Blake had found her. The pressure in her bladder grew and she needed to get to the toilet. Taking additional deep breaths in anticipation of the pain, she was going to experience she worked up the nerve and slowly began to stand. Her first attempt caused a sharp pain to go through her like a bolt of lightning, stopping her. She quickly sat back down and, determined to stand without help, Michele tried again. This time the pain was less intense as she rose to her feet but sat back down when she couldn't find her balance. Her legs were not ready to support her. She knew she had to get up, knowing she couldn't hold back the urine flow much longer. Being stubborn and determined not to let her current captures see her as weak and vulnerable, she tried again. After several more deep breathes and a loud grunt accompanied by a "goddamn it legs fucking work!", She was on her feet albeit slightly wobbly, but she was standing and knew she could get to the toilet on her own. Instinctively, she grabbed her purse and shoes from the coffee table as she slowly made her way to the toilet on her wobbly legs. Michele made sure the bathroom door was latched shut before sitting on the toilet. As she sat there, she thought she would never stop peeing. The IV fluid did its job of rehydrating her along with flushing out the drugs that she had received while tied to the bed in the shanty. After she had drained her bladder, she started to feel better right away and could think more clearly. She didn't know if she was safe or if she was still being held captive. The first thing that came to mind was she needed to escape from where she was being held and get back to the safety of the resort. She checked the bathroom window to see if it would open. Not only did the window swing open, but she also saw that the opening was large enough she could get through without a struggle. The flimsy latch on the door would not keep the door shut long enough for her to escape. Michele needed to do something to prevent anyone from coming through the door and stop her from escaping through the window. She broke both heels off her shoes and tightly wedged them under the door hoping that they would hold long enough for her to escape. Her heart started racing and her body filled with adrenaline as she grabbed her purse and heel-less shoes. She wasted no time crawling out the window into the almost empty yard. Once she was outside the house, she rushed to the street hoping to find some clue as to where she was and how to get back to the resort. Michele was halfway to the street when she heard the front door open. Michele didn't look back, she kept going and thinking to herself, *If I stop, they will get me, I got to keep going.* Sophia knew Michele wasn't going to stop because those who ran in the past never did. Standing in the open-door Sophia shouted, "You don't have to run you're safe here." As she expected, Michele didn't stop. When Michele got to the street, she had no idea which way to go to get to safety. Sophia yelled again, this time she told Michele which direction the main street was in, and the resort was just half a mile from there. Sophia wasn't worried about Michele making it back to the resort safely because while Michele was in the bathroom she called Blake's father who said he would send someone to watch over Michele while she made her way back to the resort. Sophia stood in the doorway watching until she could no longer see Michele. As she closed the front door, she said to herself, "They aways run."

Michele walked at a brisk pace as she made her way back to the resort. She tried running but being barefoot made running painfully difficult. She tried putting her shoes on but with the heels missing the shoes were useless. She reached the resort and stopped--there was no way she was going to enter through the front lobby. She didn't want to draw attention to herself. Doing her best to stay in the shadows, Michele made her way back to the deserted pool area. From here she could get to her room with minimal risk of running into staff or other guests this late at night. At the door to their room, Michele hesitated. The knot that formed in her stomach as she was about to knock on the door made her stop. She didn't know if Patty was in the room and she did not want her to see her like this. She fished around in her purse for her room key, hoping it was still there. The key was still there along with a small wad of cash she had. Michele quietly keyed her way into the room. There were no lights on and stepping in, she ran her hand up and down the wall till she found the light switch. Michele was sneaking her way to her bedroom, passing through the shared living room she noticed Patty's bedroom door was open. Michele crept over to the door to see if Patty was there. Michele felt relieved when she found Patty's room empty. Heaving a sigh of relief, Michele went to her bedroom and shut and locked the door. The adrenaline rush was wearing off, with the achiness making a fast return. With all that she had been through, Michele felt gross. It was a vile type of grossness that words couldn't begin to describe. She was experiencing the feeling that only people who went through the abuse and trauma she went through could relate to. There was a desperate need to cleanse herself. She stripped down, letting her clothing fall to the floor, and went into her bathroom. She ran the shower, allowing the water to get as hot as she could tolerate before stepping in. Once inside the shower, Michele let the water flow over her in hopes the water would wash away the grime of the evil acts they committed to her body. It only took moments for the trauma of the past few days to hit. The trauma came in the form of flashbacks so powerful they caused Michele to double over and collapse on the shower floor. She lay in the fetal position hugging herself and crying. Michele began to scream and cry out in pain. Michele wailed, "Daddy this is your fault! Why didn't you save me?!" Then there were the cries and screams of, "Where were you, Patty? Why didn't you look for me?" "OH GOD, why did you let them do this to me you bastard! why did you let them do this?!" She kept screaming until she could no longer speak. She lay there under the endless flow of hot water crying until the early hours of the morning.

Chapter 27

Blake sat in the sand and leaned up against the lifeguard shack which helped support him as he held a sleeping Patty in his arms. He couldn't stop his mind from racing with the thoughts of the insane amount of overwhelming information and events that happened that night. He was raised as an only child by his father and the nannies his father hired to take care of him. Blake, not knowing he had any siblings, then being told Mateo was his brother, blew his mind. He uncovered the truth about the rumors of female guests going missing and being sexually assaulted coupled with the fact it was a hotel employee that was behind it. The way Jeremy manipulated Mateo, and everything that went on, boggled his mind. The one thing that dominated his thoughts was what Patty had said, "I love you too, Josh." Those words stung like a piercing arrow to his heart. The woman he fell in love with, the only women he couldn't get off his mind from the moment they met, was in love with someone else.

The sun was just starting to rise over the Caribbean Sea when Blake had shifted his thoughts from what was occupying his mind to the black smoke off in the distance. The distracting smoke didn't last very long before it started to fade. Blake figured it was just an old tanker blowing off its unburned fuel oil, something that wasn't uncommon with those old ships. With the smoke now gone, Blake sat watching as the sun rose over the water waiting for Patty to wake up. When the sun had fully risen and was shining brightly in the blue, cloudless sky, was when Patty began to stir. She needed to take a moment to get her wits about her and remember that she had fallen asleep on the beach with Blake. Patty sat up and turned to Blake saying, "I'm scared. I don't know if Michele is dead or alive, I can't find her, and I don't know what to do." Blake knew Michele was safe and out of danger and as much as he wanted to tell Patty what happened he knew he couldn't. He told Patty he didn't know what they could do and suggested that he walk her back to her room so she could get cleaned up, while he went back to his place to do the same. Going back to his place was something he didn't want to do. What Blake wanted was to go back to the resort and be with her. He didn't want sex he just wanted to hold her and let the hot water from the shower relax their bodies and wash away tension from last night. Just holding her naked body against him was all he wanted but after Patty said Josh's name out loud, he knew he was only going to make things worse for himself. She was going back home in a few days to a life that didn't include him. He told her he would meet her in the small café across from the resort and talk about what to do next while they have breakfast. Patty didn't like the idea because that was time wasted when they could be looking for Michele instead of sitting in the cafe, but since she didn't know what else to do, she agreed. As they walked across the beach to the resort, Patty reached over and took Blake by the hand, resting her head on his shoulder. Blake wanted to ask her who Josh was and if she was in love with him, but he thought better of it. He already knew the answer. What he really needed to think about was how to go about getting Michele back to the resort without Patty finding out about what he knew and had done to save Michele. Blake walked Patty to the door of her room and told her he would see her in an hour. Patty asked, "before you leave will you go in with me to see if Michele has returned on her own? I really need your moral support". Blake agreed and went in with Patty. Patty called Michele's name a few times hoping to get a response. When she didn't, they went to see if she was out on the balcony, only to find that empty as well. Patty got a sinking feeling when Blake suggested trying her room. With shaking hands and tears welling up in her eyes convinced she was going to find Michele's bedroom empty, further confirming her worst fear that she was dead. Patty slowly opened the door to Michele's bedroom and whispered, "Michele are you in there?" With no response Patty peered into the dimly lit room. Her eyes filled with tears as she threw her hands over her mouth so the screech she let out wouldn't wake the sleeping Michele. Seeing the half-naked Michele sleeping on her bed was an instant emotional overload for Patty. Every single emotion imaginable came flooding through her, as she began to cry. Blake heard the barely audible screech and came rushing over to see what was going on. He looked into the room and was at a loss for words when he saw Michele sleeping in her bed. Blake didn't know Michele had escaped through the bathroom window. Sophia said she was going to monitor Michele's condition all night so why and how did Michele get back to the resort, is what he asked himself. Even though he was caught off guard he played it cool by whispering in Patty's ear, "Thank God she is back." Then he suggested that they should let her sleep, and they could talk to her when she wakes up. Patty wanted nothing more than to rush over to Michele and hug her and tell her how scared she was, but she knew Blake was right, so she quietly shut the door so Michele could sleep. When they stepped back into the living room, Blake said to Patty that Michele might need to see a familiar face when she finally woke up. He went on to say, "We don't know where she was or if anything bad happened to her. Maybe it is better if you were here when she wakes up." He was doing his best to pretend that he was oblivious to the truth. Patty thought that was a good idea and agreed. Seeing how relieved Patty was that Michele was back and safe became a reminder to Blake the Patty had family, friends, and a life that didn't include him. He also knew that there was a Josh who was part of her life and she loved him. At least that is what she said last night, "I love you too Josh." He felt that maybe this was a good time for him to quietly leave and let Patty go back to her own life knowing her trip would soon be over. He desperately wanted to tell Patty how he truly felt. He wanted to tell her he never believed in love at first sight until he met her a few days ago on the beach. He wanted to know where she was from because he wanted to transfer from Universidad Anahuac Cancun to a University near her so they could be together. Blake wanted to tell her he wasn't going to be a lifeguard forever. But he knew there was a Josh and telling her how he felt would only lead to heartbreak for him. Blake made an excuse to leave, telling Patty she needed to get some rest too and he would check in on them both later. Before Patty could respond, Blake made his exit. Patty sat on the sofa, not knowing that Blake had fallen in love with her. She sat for a while thinking about the past few days, thinking how one minute they were having a great time, and the next, their trip almost became a tragic disaster. The whole thing was so emotionally overwhelming that she began to cry, eventually crying herself to sleep.

Blake arrived back at his place shortly after leaving Patty. He wanted to go ask Sophia what happened and how did Michele get back to the resort. He knew those questions could wait, Michele was found alive, she didn't need medical attention, and she was back with Patty. Right now, he just needed to crawl into bed and sleep. He had been up for twenty-four hours and was both physically and emotionally drained. He would deal with the rest if there was anything for him to deal with, later.

Chapter 28

Exhaustion set in for the trio of Michele, Patty and Blake as all three slept through the day and into the next morning. Patty woke up in the same spot that she cried herself to sleep on. She was up before Michele and had gone ahead and ordered breakfast for both her and Michele. Patty sat out on the balcony sipping her coffee when Michele came out of her room. Michele could see the room service cart that Patty had rolled over to the sliding glass door. Her hair was still wet from the shower, and she was wrapped in a big white guest robe. The robe, although too warm to wear in the hot summer months, covered her bruised body. Besides her face, her wrist and ankles were the only places she wasn't bruised. The straps they used to tie her up were specifically designed so they would not leave marks. Michele's body still ached from the abuse and trauma she suffered which caused her to slowly creep towards the cart. Michele had a couple of aspirin in her hand that she popped into her mouth as she poured herself a cup of coffee. Michele fixed herself a plate of scrambled eggs, bacon, and toast from the cart then turned and abruptly went back to her room. Patty, feeling helpless and concerned, watched her friend pour her coffee and fix a plate for herself. Michele's expressionless face and the hallowed look in her eyes spoke volumes in the awkward silence of those few moments of watching her. Patty knew Michele had been rattled to her

core; she had never seen Michele like this. The feeling of relief she had because Michele was back was now being replaced with the same anxiety she had earlier as fear was overcoming her again. That fear she was feeling now was for the unknown. Not knowing what happened or the effects of what happened scared her. Patty had a feeling that the last few days of their trip were going to be spent in the room. She was thinking that Michele was going to keep herself locked in her bedroom. Only come out for food till it was time to head to the airport for the flight home. Michele isolating herself was another thing that scared Patty.

Later that morning Michele came out of her room. This time she wore a red silk full length jumpsuit instead of the white robe she had had on earlier that morning. The red jumpsuit reminded Patty of the jumpsuit the spokeswoman wore on that home shopping channel she loved to watch. Patty was saving up so she could buy one in black satin for herself, silk was too expensive for her. The Jumpsuit Michele had on was light and airy for summer and was perfect for hiding the bruises on her body. Her mood was different too. She seemed very relaxed, almost euphoric, and she was smiling. Michele told Patty she wanted to go shopping and explore all the different cafés and bistros in downtown Cancun. She walked up to Patty and gave her an air hug and an air kiss on her cheek saying she was sorry if she made her worry, she didn't mean to spend the night someplace else without telling her. Before Patty could open her mouth and say anything like "Just one night? You have been gone for longer than that. I thought you were dead." Which is what she was saying in her head as Michele shooed her to her room to shower and get dressed so they could get going. Michele said she didn't want to spend the rest of their trip in the room.

Blake had walked into his bedroom the prior morning and laid down on his bed with the intention of taking a nap for a few hours. He woke up the following morning in the same clothes and position he fell asleep in. He wasn't surprised that he slept that long, he was thinking about everything that went on as he got out of bed and headed for the little kitchenette to plug in the coffee maker. He went back to the bedroom to strip off yesterday's clothing and headed for the shower. The soothing water from the shower helped wake him up and feel better physically but did nothing for his heavy heart. He stepped out of the shower and wrapped the towel he used to dry off with around his waist and headed to the front door to grab the morning paper. He poured himself a cup of coffee and fixed it just the way he liked it, with a splash of cream, all the while thinking about Patty. Sitting down at his dinette table, he unfolded his newspaper to see the headline "Local fishing and tour boat catches fire and sinks killing it's Captain." The brief write-up stated, "The local tour guide everyone called Captain Jack had perished in the fire, and he was alone at the time of the fire." Blake felt his heart start to race as the nausea built in his stomach causing him to throw up a little in his mouth. He wanted those guys to pay for what they did, but not like this. He was a firm believer in the saying, "There are a lot worse fates than death." Having Captain Jack and Jeremy suffer a long slow agonizing death in a Mexican prison was a hell of a lot more punishing than an instant death. He honestly believed that people would rather die than go to a Mexican prison and he wasn't wrong to believe that the Mexican prisons lived up to their reputation. Reading this story was raising his ire. Normally he is an even-keeled person, not too much in the world upset him. Killing Captain Jack upset him in the worst way imaginable. He felt betrayed by Amelia after he was told by her that he could trust Pauly and that he knew what to do. He thought to himself that if he knew Pauly was going to do this, he would never have trusted him. He would have found another way. Yes, they were monsters for what they had done. Yes, there is an unknown number of innocent women who are now permanently scarred for life. But just killing them, without bringing them to justice, without letting them suffer and rot in the notorious Mexican prison system where they would have truly paid for their crimes, and to have Pauly betray his trust like that was the trigger that brought out his anger. Blake read the story repeatedly. Each time he read the words that were printed on the page in front of him, his outrage grew. He became so irate that when he pushed himself away from the table to get up, the chair he was sitting in toppled over backwards and slammed the back of the chair on the floor. He didn't realize the towel he had wrapped around his waist had fallen off when the chair had fallen over. Blake, now completely naked, angrily stormed off to the bedroom. He quickly threw on whatever clothes he could find. He grabbed the newspaper off the kitchenette table as he went storming out the front door. He needed to confront Amelia about Pauly.

The girls discovered a small sidewalk bakery that had the most amazing tres leches cake according to the sign in the window. They both ordered a slice of cake and a café de olla to go with their cake. Michele had taken two more little white pills out of her tiny handbag and popped them into her mouth, with a sip of the hot beverage that she thought was "to die" for. "Never before have I had a coffee that tasted this wonderful, the spices are simply delightful." She said to Patty after swallowing the pills and the liquid she used to wash them down. Patty was giving Michele the look that asked a question without using words. It was the same look her mother would give her when she knew Michele was up to no good and wanted to know what was going on without having to ask. Michele sheepishly grinned and said, "What, they're just aspirin." Taking Michele at her word, Patty went back to her cake and drinking her spiced coffee that she had to agree with Michele, was the best cup of coffee she had ever had. By the time they finished, Michele was feeling the effects of the white pills and was ready to do more shopping and explore more of the food venues. They passed a clothing shop and, in the front window was a mannequin dressed in a tailor-made button-down shirt with a tropical pattern, white linen beach pants, sandals and a Panama Jack fedora with a solid black band at the base of the crown where the crown meets the brim. "Cowabunga check out those threads." Michele joyfully exclaimed as she grabbed Patty's arm

to get her to stop and look at the outfit. "My Joshy would look so gnarly-
-no wait, he would look so radically gnarly sporting that gear." In her
mind Patty was thinking *Joshy? Sporting that gear? What's in that
aspirin she's taking? Would the real Michele Gibson please stand up.*
Michele was not herself; she was never this bubbly or had ever called
Josh, her Joshy. Patty didn't know what to think but she liked the way
Michele was acting. It was a pleasant change from the Michele she
knew. No sooner than Michele got the words out of her mouth, her
attention quickly shifted and was now focused on the small café across
the street. She could smell the aroma of beef being cooked on the
kitchens grill causing her stomach to grumble as if it was saying,
"FEED ME!" Patty heard the sounds coming from Michele's belly and
began to laugh. Both girls looked at one another, knowing what the
other was thinking, giggled, then turned and went to the little café for
lunch. They asked the waiter what smelled so good. He told him it was
their special of the day Carne asada served with rice and beans and a
free house margarita. Both girls ordered the special; who would pass up
free margaritas? They continued with their shopping spree after their
lunch. Although the food absorbed most of the alcohol, Michele, as
Patty's father would say, was acting a little loopy, which made Patty
aware that those pills were something more than just aspirin. Michele
has always been able to handle alcohol or smoking pot without getting
all silly and goofy like she is now. Michele was mellow but at the same
time she had a skip to her step and was singing, "What's Love Got to
do With It" and saying she loves the 'teens', which was her silly way of

saying she loved Tina Turner. Michele was displaying a certain euphoria that Patty had not seen before.

Blake arrived at Amelia's and was slightly out of breath from rushing to get there. He didn't have to knock at the door Amelia heard his stomping as he marched up the walkway. Blake barged right in without waiting to be invited. After shutting the door, Amelia calmly said, "I saw the headline in this morning's paper too." Blake shouted, "What the fuck Amelia, I thought I could trust you!" Still using a calm voice, "Keep your voice down. Matty doesn't know what happened here last night. I gave him something to help him sleep and he is still sleeping." "I'm awake madre. What happened? Did you save the girl? Did you find the three bad men?" Blake forgot about there being a third person involved. When he saw what was going on in the shanty and who it was, he was so angered by what he saw the two doing he completely forgot that Mateo told him there were three men in the shanty. *Amburo! That bastard, how could I have forgotten?* immediately ran through Blake's mind. Mateo's question broke the tension in the room, giving Amelia the opportunity she needed to calm Blake down and explain she had no idea what Pauly was going to do, and where he was. She figured he would have gone to Blake's father's house after torching the boat. She thought that even though the newspaper said Captain Jack was alone on the boat, Pauly put Jeremy on the boat too. Being offshore, he was betting no one would find the other body. Since Jeremy had no family, no one would miss him or come looking for him. Amelia took a few minutes to explain to him that she had no idea what Pauly was going to do but also was glad that what he was doing would protect Mateo. There was no way any of them could talk now and take down Mateo by trying to spin the narrative to make it look like Mateo was behind it. No one would buy that story, but she couldn't let Mateo go through that; he wouldn't be able to handle it. Blake didn't want to hear what Amelia had to say; he just wanted to know where Amburo lived so he could try and find him before he got away or before Pauly got to him. He told Amelia that he believed her, not that he really did, but because that is what she wanted him to believe. If he said he believed her then maybe by telling her what she wanted to hear, she would tell him where Amburo lived. Blake hoped he would get to him before he fled or before Pauly got to him. It worked. As soon as Amelia heard what she wanted to hear, she told him what he wanted to know. As Blake headed for the door, Amelia shouted to him not to forget his promise about protecting Mateo and that he needed to do whatever it took to protect him. Hoping her words didn't fall on deaf ears, she began praying for Mateo's safety.

Blake ran to the location he was given by Amelia. As Blake was approaching the property, he slowed his pace down to a walk. He was in the seedy side of town; the area Patty had told him she was in the other night when she ventured out to look for Michele. Being there during the day was scary enough --he couldn't imagine what this place was like at night. He didn't know if Patty was brave or crazy for coming here, but it did show just how much she was willing to do for her best friend. Ironically, he started wondering what she would do for this Josh person she said she loved. He was lost in thought when he heard an irritating squeaking noise that was like hearing fingernails on a chalk board. Coming towards him was a homeless man pushing his squeaky wheeled and wobbly old shopping cart. The cart contained the man's entire life's belongings including the snappy little Chihuahua dog oddly enough, named Snappy. The squeak, squeak of the cart and yap yap of the little ankle biter, broke the dead silence of the eerie street. The man was obviously unbathed, and his body odor could have choked a horse. He smelled of old booze, vomit, and stale urine. The front of his vomit-stained tee shirt still had a few chunks of the dinner he pulled out of a dumpster. The man flashed a huge grin which revealed the remnants of what use to be teeth at one point. He kept saying, "Watch out! Snappy is gonna get ya! He's finna to eat ya! Snappy is gonna get ya, he's finna to eat ya!" Blake never heard someone say "finna" and he assumed the man was trying to say fixing, but his oral dilemma made talking difficult. The homeless man kept saying the phrase repeatedly, even though he was well past Blake and no one else was there to hear him. Shaking his head, Blake had no idea what to make of the encounter. Turning his attention to the dark house he was standing in front of, thinking, *this must be the wrong address,* the house looked like it hadn't been lived in for years. The curtains were drawn tight, the yard unkept and overgrown with weeds and the overflowing mailbox had him thinking Amelia played him. Reluctantly entering the yard, Blake walked up to the front door and banged on it, checking to see if someone was home. When no one answered the door, he tried harder again this time so his knocking would be loud enough to be heard if they were sleeping. Still no answer. He walked around to the back of the house to see if there was a window he could look through thinking that maybe Pauly got here first. Blake cautiously made his way to the back of the house, finding a small stoop and back entrance. Hoping the door was unlocked so he could gain access, he walked up the steps of the stoop and tried to open the door. The handle turned with ease, but the door wouldn't budge it felt like something was holding the door shut. There was a window next to the door, and like the other windows, the curtains were drawn tight, but unlike the other windows, the lock on this one was broken. Fearing the broken lock was the work of Pauly, Blake opened the window only to be knocked back by the horrendously pungent odor coming from inside the house. It was an odor he knew all too well. Odor or no odor, he had to go inside. Using a trick he saw on a cop show, he used his fingers to pinch his nose closed so he would only breathe through his mouth. With his free hand he opened the curtain and climbed through the window and into the kitchen. The first thing he noticed was a mouse feasting on the remains of Amburo's mother with her hand still clutching a pair of panties and a bra. He looked around the room and saw a kitchen chair had been wedged under the door handle of the door. He tried to shove open. Removing the chair, he made sure the door could open before going to check the rest of the house. Before heading through the kitchen into the other areas of the house, he shooed the little mouse away from the dead body, sending it scurrying out the door. This time there was no cat in the yard giving the mouse safe passage to his nest. Blake started to make his way into the rest of the small house and didn't have to travel far before he came across another kitchen chair. This time the chair was tipped over and above the chair was Amburo, with a noose around his neck.

An already shaken Amburo arrived home shortly after leaving the shanty. He thought he had killed the girl held captive by him and his accomplices. Entering the house he shared with his mother through the back door, she confronted Amburo as he entered the kitchen. She was standing in the center of the room holding Amburo's trophy, Michele's bra and panties. Amburo had kept the under garments of their victims, treating their clothing as his prized possessions. He saw her holding his prizes that he kept hidden from her, and she was shouting at him in their native tongue, "What have you done? Why would you do this to these girls?" He instantly filled with rage. She was shaking her fist with the balled up under garments at Amburo, with tears streaming down her cheeks, she shouted at him, "Have you forgotten what they did to me? You have become just like soldiers? You monster!" Amburo answered in his mind, *I do remember how weak I was.* He replied through gritted teeth "I do remember how I was too much of a coward to protect my own mother. I am no longer a coward; I am strong, STRONG, just like the soldiers!". Amburo's fury grew as his mother kept shaking her clenched hand at him yelling, "You monster! You Monster!" until his inner rage turned into a violent attack on her. Amburo, blinded by his rage, grabbed his mother wrapping both hands around her neck. His grip was getting tighter and his mother was struggling to get air into her lungs, unable to escape. Fear gripped her harder than her son's hands.

Severe pain and pressure grew in her neck and temples as her lungs screamed for oxygen. The last thing she heard was a loud baritone scream coming from deep within her son as he lifted her off the floor by her neck. She felt his hand quickly shift as her neck let out a loud crack and in a split second she was gone. Amburo let out soul purging scream that snapped him out of his blind rage and back into the moment. He saw his mother's lifeless body dangling from his hands. He was looking at his dead mother's body with disbelief as the shocking realization overcame him that he had just killed his mother. His mind became as lifeless as his mother's body. He released his grip, dropping her to the floor. Without a thought going through his mind and a stare as blank as a sheet of paper, he grabbed two chairs from the kitchen table. He used one to firmly brace the exterior kitchen door shut. He brought the second one into the tiny gathering room with the exposed ceiling and set the chair in the center of the room. He made sure the front door's dead bolt was engaged, to make sure no one could stop him. He went to his bedroom and stripped the top sheet from his bed. He twisted the sheet tight, so it resembled a rope. He went back out to the gathering room with his makeshift rope and tied one end around his neck. Then, standing tiptoed on the chair, he securely attached the other end to the exposed beam in the ceiling above. He slowly started to lower himself from the tiptoed position as the rope tightened around his neck. There was no slack left in the rope and the tension grew on his neck. Amburo managed to kick the chair out from under him as he welcomed his instant death. Suspended by the noose around his neck the instant death he wanted did not come and he was now faced with a long, slow agonizing death. Within seconds, panic set in overwhelming him with fear as his primal flight or fight response kicked in. He didn't want to die after all, at least not like this. With the weight of his own body compressing the noose around his neck, he could feel the pain and pressure immensely intensified and became frightened that he could not draw air into his lungs. Like his mother, his body began screaming for oxygen; his heart was pounding so hard it was if it were trying to break free from his rib cage. Frantically, he violently clawed at the noose to free himself. His fingernails gouged deeply into his neck, turning the noose from the white bedsheet red from his blood. Amburo desperately struggled to save his own life from a self-inflicted and horrifying death. The pressure in his eyes grew, his vision blurred, and white spots replaced the ceiling he could no longer see. Dizziness and confusion took over his mind as his bladder and bowels began releasing. The minutes turned into what seemed like hours as he started to fade into the blackness of the abyss. Hours had passed while his body hung limp and lifeless. Amburo drifted in and out of consciousness. The house, now cast into darkness from nightfall, and the curtains tightly closed, even the outside light from the streetlamps could not filter into the house. He hung there waiting for death to take him. Amburo heard a banging coming from the back door bringing him back to a state of semi-consciousness. Hanging there in the darkness, he realized help was here. He tried to gather what strength he could to scream loud enough for the person at the back door to hear him. He struggled to lift his arms so he could loosen the noose enough to get a breath, hoping he could be heard. Amburo's attempts to scream and struggle were in vain; his entire body jerked one final time, then he went limp, as death won the battle. The ceiling joist that Amburo had tied the sheet to creaked loudly as his body jerked for that last time. Patty had taken a step back at the same time the ceiling joist made its death rattle on Amburo's behalf, but thought it was the old wooden stoop making the noise as she stepped away from the door. Patty headed back to the street unaware of the scene straight out of a horror movie was just on the other side of the door.

Blake stood there in the gathering room not knowing if the clawing marks on Amburo's neck were from a botched suicide attempt, or if Pauly was the one who did this. Blake picked up the fallen chair so he could get a look at Amburo's neck. He was a lifeguard by day and an undergrad student of forensic science at the University. He knew the rope markings on a victim's neck would hold clues for him to tell if Amburo committed suicide or if this was staged to look like a suicide to cover up a murder. A quick look was all he needed to know that this wasn't staged. Blake climbed down from the chair and placed it back the way he had found it. The smell of body decomposition and the fowl stench of urine and human excrement was getting to him. The mouth breathing trick did not work as well as he wanted it. He then left the same way he came in, not forgetting to secure the back door with the chair the way Amburo had. Back out in the street he stood staring at the house thinking he needed to call the Federales, but he knew he couldn't because the crime scene contained his fingerprints. He knew his father had influence over the local officials and he wouldn't get into trouble, but this would be a mess his father would want to know about before anyone else.

Chapter 29

The girls arrived back to their room with enough time to shower and change for the resort's beach barbeque and bonfire event. Michele went into her bedroom and threw her purse and shopping bags on her bed and headed straight for the shower. Patty waited for Michele to get into the shower before she sneaked into Michele's room to see what those pills were. She found a pill bottle, but the label was in Spanish, making her wish she had paid attention and didn't cheat off Michele in their high school Spanish class. When Michele had locked herself in the bathroom at Amelia's house, she had quickly rifled through Amelia's medicine cabinet. She was looking for something to stop the pain before climbing out of the bathroom window. Michele had found a bottle with white pills in it. The label was in Spanish, but she did recognize the word opioide, the Spanish word for opioid. Michele took the bottle with her. Michele had taken a Quaalude as a dare in the past knowing it was an opioid. She did experience the euphoric effect but instead of relaxing Michele, like the drug is supposed to do, the drug had a much different effect on her. It did relax her in a euphoric sense but didn't make her drowsy and she became happier, even perky. In that moment in front of Amelia's medicine cabinet, she knew that the contents of that pill bottle would make all the pain away. Patty put the pills back but not before being caught. Patty didn't hear Michele step out of the shower and open the bathroom door stepping into the doorway with nothing on except that devilish grin she would get when she wanted something. Michele startled Patty when she said, "Hey I was just coming to get you. I want you to join me in the shower." Patty spun around with the bottle still in her hand. Patty stood wide- eyed, staring at Michele with a gaping mouth. She was shocked by all the bruises that were on Michele's body. Momentarily frozen in place, Patty was dumbfounded by what she saw. Michele, still under the effects of the pills, cat walked over to Patty and wrapped her arms around her and snuggled up to Patty whispering in her ear, "Let's just put that back in the bag and come join me in the shower."   Michele slid one of her hands down the front of Patty till she reached her thigh then started to slide her hand up Patty's skirt trying to get her friend all hot and bothered. The rubbing of Michele's hand on her thigh was enough to snap Patty back into the moment. Patty, who had never been attracted to women, was now faced with the opportunity to be alone with Michele, which was something she wanted but the circumstances were all wrong. She only wanted to be with Michele so she could get to Josh. "Michele, those bruises. What happened to you?" Michele didn't answer Patty she just kept rubbing Patty's thigh. Patty was in the middle of her monthly hell week, and Michele was inches away from finding that out. Patty told Michele, "Please just stop."

Trying to wiggle free from Michele, Patty asked again, "What happened to you? What are these pills?" But Michele just kept up the rubbing and started kissing the nape of Patty's neck. That was the spot that always made Patty wet but not this time. A frustrated Patty demanded Michele to stop and stepped away from Michele. "Okay, Okay chillax bitch! Nothing happened, I'm fine. So stop asking me what happened." Michele reached up and took the pills from Patty and threw them back into her purse. Patty now is more demanding with her tone. "No! Look at you, you're not fine. Who did this to you?" Michele, not wanting to talk about it, tried changing the subject. She started to catwalk back to the bathroom, telling Patty if she dropped the subject, she would make it worth her while. Patty refused to drop the questioning. Patty, not knowing what happened to her, could tell by the number of bruises and the pills she was taking, Michele had been brutally assaulted and violated. Patty was horrified to think that this is the stuff nightmares were made of. Patty didn't ask, she demanded Michele tell her what happened. Patty raised her voice and demanded to know what happened to her. This triggered Michele's defenses. Michele didn't want to talk about it, and goddamn it, she wasn't going to talk about it if she didn't want to. Michele spun around, and the look on her face could have stopped a bullet. The look was all Patty needed to see. She knew that the conversation was over, and over permanently. She was to never speak of Michele's disappearance, the bruises, or the pills ever again. No words needed to be said; the look said what words couldn't.

The front gate was open, and the guard told Blake to go right up to the house as his father was expecting him. The house Blake spent his childhood in was enormous. The well-kept grounds were spectacular. They were filled with lush greenery, fountains, patios, and pond-like pools filled with exotic fish. The swimming pool with sundecks were strategically placed around the grounds to give guests optimal views of the Caribbean Sea yet were close enough to the house so the help could easily service guests from the outdoor commercial style kitchen. As beautiful as it was, Blake hated growing up here; he much preferred a smaller cozier home. He took after his mother in that sense. He was met at the front door by one of the caretakers who told him his father was in his office and to go right in. Blake entered the large room with its solid Mahogany walls and lush Teak accents. The two exotic woods were seamlessly joined together and painstakingly handcrafted by some of Mexico's finest craftsmen. The large fireplace surrounded by solid wood bookcases added to the touch of elegance yet gave the room a warm feeling in addition to the exotic woods. His father was seated in his high-backed, leather, reading chair and was flanked by Pauly who was to his left. "I know why you are here." said his father as Blake approached. "Did you do the same to Jeremy?" Blake asked. Blake was carefully choosing his words and using those words wisely. You never directly accuse the Cartel even if you were blood. "Sit, let's talk," his father said. Reluctantly, Blake sat on the leather sofa across from his father. Before Blake could say anything, his father said, "Don't be angry with Pauly, he was just doing as I ordered. I had to protect the family business." Blake said nothing in return. One of the unspoken rules is you never speak when El Jefe is talking business. Pauly never failed to follow that rule; however, today was different. Today El Jefe needed to do whatever it took to make all this go away. Pauly was the man who could get what needed to be done and done without leaving evidence behind that could implicate any of Cartel members. English was Pauly's second language which he spoke poorly. Even though he spoke English more than he did Spanish, he asked, "Dónde está el hombre negro?" Pauly spoke in his native tongue when he needed to be dead serious. Rounding up all three men was as serious as it got. Blake, who was raised bilingual, understood the question; he told Pauly and his father about the murder suicide. When Blake had finished telling his father and Pauly about what he found inside Amburo's house, the three men sat in silence for what felt like an eternity to Blake. He broke the silence by again asking about Jeremy. His father said Jeremy was alive and was being held in a room in the basement. Then his father told Blake what he planned to do with Jeremy and how Blake was going to carry out his plan. When Blake heard he was going to be the one to take care of Jeremy, he wanted to stand up to his father and tell him no. Instead he listened to his plan in hopes it would honor his late mother's wishes. Blake breathed a sigh of relief when his father had finished telling Blake the plan which include protecting Mateo and his mother.

Chapter 30

Blake had always known he was going to leave Cancun one day, but he never really made plans to leave, nor did he want to leave before finishing University. He was thinking he could move to Mexico City in hopes of becoming a forensic investigator for Mexico's Secretary of Security and Civilian Protection as a liaison in California's Department of Justice's CBI field office located in southern California. He surely didn't want to leave this way. He could no longer consider Blake Sr, a father. The truth about him being the El Hefe of a ruthless Cartel destroyed what little semblance of a father figure he had, and no longer was he able to call him Padre. Hearing the plan El Hefe had laid out, Blake realized it was time to leave; this was the best way to honor his mother's wishes. Blake was rushing to pack with barely enough time to gather the few belongings he owned and get back to El Hefe so he could carry out the plan. El Hefe was right, not only was this in the best interest of the Cartel's business, which was the part of the plan he loathed, but he made a promise to Amelia, and by carrying out the plan he would be able to keep that promise. In the end, he knew he was doing the right thing for Mateo, Amelia, and himself. There was not enough time to say goodbye to Patty, but that didn't seem to matter. Before long, he would be forgotten, only to become a faded and distant memory. Blake was unaware that Josh was Michele's boyfriend and Patty was falling in love with him. However, Patty did say "I love you too Josh." To Blake that was all the convincing he needed to understand he was just another notch in some random girl's bedpost. Standing in the tiny house taking one last look at the place he proudly called home for the past few years, Blake said, "I will be the man Padre could never be. I will make you proud Madre I will make you proud." Blake was proud of the place he could call his own because he rented this small furnished house without the help of El Hefe. This was a house that represented not only independence, but also freedom from the grasp El Hefe would have held over him, had it not been for his mother. She was the only person El Hefe could never say no to. With one last look around and a heavy sigh, Blake picked up the last of his belongings and headed for the door to start a new life.

Regardless of the earlier tension in Michele's bedroom, the girls had the time of their lives at the bonfire. They feasted on freshly caught fish cooked over an open fire pit along with many other appetizing and mouthwatering Mexican delicacies. The music was loud and everyone danced on the beach around the fire. Patty saw just how much fun Michele was having and began to think that maybe she overreacted, and the bruising wasn't as bad as she thought. Later that night when they arrived back in their room, they both sat in the living room on the sofa laughing and talking about the food, how great the band was and the fun everyone had. When they finally settled down a bit, Patty turned to Michele and said she was sorry about what happened earlier in the bedroom. She told Michele she felt bad because she really did want to join her in the shower even if Auntie Flow was still doing her thing. Michele turned to Patty, smiled then leaned in and started kissing Patty. At first Patty just savored the moment. She wasn't sure if she would like it because she was not attracted to women but was enjoying kissing the person she looked up to--the person she idolized growing up. She was glad that she was enjoying it because she was eager to take things further now, she knew the idea of the threesome would work and she was finally going to get Josh inside her. Patty slid her hand down Michele's thigh and then into her crotch gently rubbing Michele through the linen beach pants she wore to the bonfire. Patty started to massage the bruised area in Michele's crotch, the area that always gave Michele great pleasure. But tonight, it caused Michele immense discomfort, so much so that Michele quickly brushed Patty's hand away. Fortunately for Michele, she was still under the effects of the pills which masked most of the pain, making it easy for Michele to hide her discomfort. Michele quickly interlocked her finger with the hand she brushed away and told Patty she just wanted to kiss for now. As much as Michele wanted Patty to fondle her, the pills had worn off just enough to make her realize sex would be too painful and she needed time to heal. The girls eventually moved the kissing to Michele's room where they kissed and cuddled for a while before falling asleep. Later that night Michele experienced a nightmare that jolted her awake just before daybreak. She dreamt that she was still tied to the bed in the shanty. In the dream she wasn't blindfolded, and she could see the faceless men who were standing over her. The three men had featureless flesh-colored faces no eyes, no noses, no mouths just a blank patch of skin where their face should have been. They were talking to her, but she couldn't understand what they were trying to say through the mouthless blob of a face. The men's faces would zoom in close to her face then zoom back out each time one of them tried to speak. Then it was as if the three of them melded together and formed one giant monster blob that started raping her. That was when her eyes popped open, and she woke up from her nightmare. She lay there next to Patty staring up at the ceiling trying to regain her wits. Grounding herself, she quietly got out of bed and went to her purse to get the little white pills. Without disturbing Patty, she quietly went into the bathroom, shut the door, took her pills, and then stepped into the shower. The girls finished packing and said goodbye to Cancun as they left for the airport to fly back home. Unbeknownst to the girls, they were being escorted by one of the Cartel members who was there to ensure their safety. They were in mid-flight when Patty started to gently rub Michele's hand that was on the arm rest. Glancing over at Michele, she smiled and gave Michele an affectionate wink. Patty told Michele she liked kissing her. Michele sat silently as Patty suggested maybe they could do more next time. After a few moments of silence Michele told Patty, "Everything that happened in Cancun stays in Cancun." Michele turned to Patty. "And I do mean everything." Michele once again gave Patty that look that could stop a bullet, but this time Michele's eyes had an evilness to them and for the first time in all the years they were friends, Michele scared Patty. Patty took her hand off Michele's and cowered back in her seat the rest of the flight home. The flight home was a direct flight to Bangor's International Airport. The direct flight landed on time, and as promised, Josh was at the baggage claim waiting to pick the girls up.

Blake's father was reluctant to agree to let Blake walk back to his house from the now vacant house but knew Blake needed to do this for himself. He knew Blake needed the long walk to do what he needed to do mentally to prepare himself. Blake slowly walked towards his destination with the two duffle bags that contained what little he owned when he heard the sirens of Cancun's fire department heading towards him. When the firetrucks came into view, he saw that they were not making any effort to race to the scene of the fire. The firetrucks casually drove past him; he turned in the direction they were going and saw smoke coming from the slums and was quick to discern where they were headed and why they were not in any rush to get there. Blake arrived at El Hefe's house to find El Hefe standing next to van that looked like the van from the T.V. show he loved to watch with the four Vietnam Vets who were wanted men but real-life heroes to the oppressed. The van's engine was already running, and the side door was open, which was El Hefe's way of saying there is going to be no long goodbye just get going. Blake thew the two duffle bags into the van, shut the sliding door and walked around to the driver's side to where El

Hefe was standing. El Hefe told him, "After you deliver the package, you will be free to go and start your new life" For the first time ever, Blake saw a tear in the eye of El Hefe, telling him that for the first time in his life, his father loved him more than he could ever comprehend. "My son" he said, "Make your madre proud live the life she wanted you to live and never look back." He finished with "I love you my son and I am proud of what you did for the girl." With tears in his eyes, the head of Mexico's largest and most powerful Cartel threw his arms around the son from the woman he could never stop loving. Blake hugged the man who was the Padre he loved, the Padre who for the first time in his life told Blake he loved him. It was the first time Blake ever saw him as a father, and the first time he saw Blake Sr. as something other than a cold hard man. It was the first time Blake felt the warmth and compassion of a loving dad. The dad who Blake's mother loved with all her heart and soul. This was the man with whom Blake's mother had fallen in love with, the man he truly was. Hugging his dad was something Blake had not done before. Both father and son, not wanting to let go, held each other tightly, appreciative of their final goodbye. With a heavy sigh, Blake's father released his embrace telling his son to be well and kissing his forehead before walking away with a heavy heart. Blake understood at that moment that besides losing his wife, this was the most difficult thing his father had ever experienced. With a heavy sigh of his own, he said, "I love you too, dad." Blake wiped his own tears away, climbed into the driver's seat, and slowly drove towards the front gate. Blake took a left turn after leaving the compound and headed towards Route 180. On his way out of town, he drove past the sand dunes that led to the shanty. The smoke coming from the area told Blake Pauly did his job and did it well. Fire had a way of destroying the things that could be used against someone. All the evidence of what the three men had done was gone.

Blake drove almost nonstop till he got to the spot where he was to drop off the package. Still inside Mexico, Blake pulled into an old, abandoned Pemex gas station. He pulled past the islands that once housed the old crank-style gas pumps and to the back of the old, white and red-striped, sun-faded building. The large glass picture windows on the front of the building were smashed, and the interior was vandalized by what appeared to be drunken teenagers looking for a place to party in hopes of getting into the pants of the female party goers. Blake continued to drive around the building to the back where there was a brown Chevy Blazer flashing its headlights. Blake slowly approached, using caution even though his gut was telling him this was the person he is supposed to deliver the package too. The driver's door to the brown Chevy Blazer opened with Jed Calhoun stepping out. Jed donned the usual outfit of cowboy boots, Wrangler jeans, a Stetson-style hat, and a brown-and-tan western shirt featuring a gold star above the heart on the left side. Jed, as they say, was a "Probie" back in sixty-two when he first joined the Texas Rangers. In those days, Jed had an addiction that wasn't chemical; Jed was a gambling addict. Jed had gotten himself in debt, a debt he would never be able to repay on a Texas Ranger's salary. One of Jed's gambling trips to Vegas landed him in hot water with a certain Casino boss. The Casino Jed would frequent was just off the main strip. Being a Texas Ranger, it was best for him to remain low key and frequenting the smaller Casinos off the main strip was ideal. It was the winter of sixty-five that the owner of the Casino got tired of waiting for Jed to pay back his debt. The moment Jed stepped through the front door of the Casino was the same moment he found out being a Texas Ranger didn't protect him from his debts, nor did it protect him from Bakarne Jaun Diaz a young up-and-coming member of the Mexican Cartel who was making a name for himself running the Casino's the Cartel used to launder their drug money and distribute their product. Bakarne was given orders to break both of Jed's arms to send the message to Jed that you pay up or the pay back will be worse. Bakarne had a better idea. Bakarne, being a visionary had a vision for a forgotten piece of land the was shaped like a seven with beautiful beaches and endless views of the Caribbean Sea. Bakarne's vision of resorts being built there was laughed at by the Cartel heads, but Bakarne saw something they didn't. He saw that he could move the operations back to Mexico, giving them unlimited access to the border as well as the protection at the border they needed from the Texas Rangers. He would also have the protection the Cartel provided inside of the Mexican Government. This move would give the Cartel a homecourt advantage. By gaining an inside man with the Texas Rangers, the Cartel would be able to move their product across the border without any interference from the law on the Texas side. Jed was given an offer he couldn't refuse, because if he refused and didn't pay back the debt, his new wife and unborn child would pay the price. Jed became the inside mole for the Cartel, and two years later, the resort city of Cancun, Mexico emerged from the isolated sand dunes, on the island, shaped like a seven, in Mexico's Yucatan Peninsula. Blake brought the van to a stop after pulling slightly past Jed. The package he was carrying was in the back of the van. As Blake was getting out of the van, Jed asked if he had the package and did it arrive in one piece. Blake nodded and went to the back of the van, opening the double doors so Jed could have a look at the package. One look at the it was enough for Jed to say, "Boy you just made a hero out of me." He told Blake that bringing Jeremy Philips in and having him stand trial for the murder of Patrica Trixie Jones was going to get him that promotion he had been longing for. Jeremy was hog-tied and gagged in the back of the van, crying and trying to beg through his gagged mouth to be let go. Jed nor Blake were going to do that; Jeremy was going to get what was coming to him. He was going to get tried and convicted and spend his remaining years in the general population having the things he did to those women done to him before being sent to death row where he would wait to be executed, if the other prisoners let him live long enough to see that day. There was no way around it; the system was already rigged against Jeremy, his fate was already signed, sealed, and delivered. Once Blake and Jed had secured Jeremy in the back of the Blazer, they went over the cover story of how Jeremy was captured before Jed handed over an oversized envelope that contained three sets of official court documents. These were the official documents giving Blake, Amelia, and Mateo their US citizenship. Getting into the Blazer to head back to El Paso, Jed shook his head and said to Blake, "I don't know how you pulled it off, but I'm impressed with the deal you made with the Cartel.". He said, "Damn son, you did the impossible." Then drove off with the package that guaranteed him the promotion that would secure his retirement from the Cartel and the Texas Rangers.

Blake sat in the driver's seat of the van waiting. It was right around dusk when a white cargo van arrived. Pauly pulled up alongside Blake, rolled down the driver's side window, and apologized for being late, telling Blake he had to wrap up a few loose ends. Blake figured the fires were the loose ends he was talking about, but he didn't know that El Hefe had Pauly drive the girls to the airport to make sure the girls got on their flight safely. That was the loose end. El Hefe ordered Pauly to make sure no one else at the resort was involved, and the girls were safe. Pauly stepped out of the van and opened the passenger door to let Mateo and Amelia out; the two were happy to see Blake. Blake and Pauly loaded their belongings from the white van into the van Blake was driving. Pauly wished them all a good life and told Blake his father was proud of him for sticking up for and protecting his brother. Pauly decided this was the right time to say, "I am proud of you for protecting our brother and being the man, I will never be". Without further delay, Pauly jumped back into the white van and sped off in the direction he came from. Amelia sat in the passenger seat next to Blake while Mateo sat in the back seat behind Amelia. Blake was putting the van into gear to drive off when Amelia reached over and putting her hand on his arm she said. "Thank you." Blake nodded before asking, "Our brother?", he shook his head and finished putting the van in drive. All three were heading to Coranado, California. The little beach town was just across the bridge from San Diego where they would settle into their new life. Blake was able to transfer to the University of California at San Diego to finish school. Amelia and Mateo would start their new positions at one of the local beach resorts.

Chapter 31

Josh sat quietly by himself in the basement of his parents' house staring at the blank TV screen, wondering what happened. He picked Michele and Patty up at the airport as promised. He told Michele how much he missed her and wanted to hear all about their trip. He was planning on taking Michele to that floating restaurant in Old Port she always wanted to go to, telling her his special girl deserves a special welcome home dinner, but Michele seemed aloof. He could see the distance in her eyes. It was like she detached herself from the world around her. Then there were those occasions when she was like her old self but still showed no interest in being his girlfriend. A month after Michele had returned from their trip, she and Josh were alone by the pool and had just finished smoking a joint. Weed made Michele horny and Josh was already getting that feeling that told him he was just one kiss away from pitching a tent. He looked over at Michele and could tell just by looking at her that the weed was doing its thing. He took her by the hand and said, "let's take a swim", and walked over to the pool stairs, where he slid his speedo off showing her his boner, telling her little Josh missed her. Josh started kissing Michele and untying her string bikini. With his free hand he guided Michele's hand to his crotch. He liked it when Michele stroked him before he slid himself into her. With her bottom now off, Josh slid his hand between her legs and to the spot he knew would get Michele going. Once he hit that spot Michele immediately pushed him away and yelled, "Don't touch me there!" She turned and ran away from him yelling, "I don't want to see you anymore! You need leave." Josh stood there asking himself, *did she just break up with me and why? What did I do?* He was more stunned and shocked than he was upset. The light tapping on the sliding glass door brought Josh back into the moment. He looked over and saw Patty waving at him, he motioned for her to come in. She sat down next to Josh and told him she tried to talk to Michele like he asked and find out why Michele wouldn't take his call. Josh was hoping to find out why she didn't want to see him anymore. Before Patty left, after not getting an answer out of Michele, Michele once again told Patty, "What happened in Mexico stays in Mexico." Josh was leaning forward on the rickety old sofa with his elbows on his knees and chin resting in his hands. Patty told Josh she tried her best and was sorry that she couldn't get an answer as she put her arm around Josh and gave him a supportive hug. Wanting Josh was the last thing on Patty's mind. She saw how upset he was and hated seeing him this way. She knew it was a supportive friend that he needed right now.

In the weeks before Michele was to move into the dorm at State University, she found out her ordeal in Mexico wasn't over. She was sitting on the toilet in her bathroom staring at what she had been waiting hours to get the results of. The pregnancy test that she drove to Massachusetts to buy because she didn't want anyone in this, as she would say, "shitbag town" to know she might be pregnant, was showing that she tested positive. Michele wasn't consistent with taking her daily dose when it came to her birth control pill making it hard for her to figure out who the father was. The baby's father could have been Josh, or the guys in the band whom she had sex with in the van along with her cousin, or if one of her rapists was the father. She couldn't be sure who got her pregnant but that still didn't stop her from being convinced it was one of the guys who raped her. There was the one thing she did know: there was no way in hell she was having a rapist's baby. If it was Josh's baby, which she doubted, she still didn't want the baby because she was going to dump him anyway. She knew she needed to go see her cousin in Canada before Lily left to study abroad in Italy. She was the one person who could help her get an abortion and never tell anyone. Later that day, Michele made the travel arrangements she needed and packed a bag for her early morning flight the next day. This time there was going to be no lovemaking with her cousin and no fun with anyone because Michele didn't want anyone to touch her that way. The emotional trauma of what happened made sex impossible for her. She tried to tell herself she needed a break from sex and that she should focus on college, but she knew that wasn't true.

The day all three had been waiting their entire senior year of high school and all summer for was finally here. It was move-in day at both

State University and Mercy College. Michele was quick to settle into her dorm. Her new roommate, who was an athlete participating on both the women's field hockey and basketball teams, meant she was hardly ever in the room. That's something Michele liked, she wasn't opposed to making some new friends and trying the whole college experience, but she did need some solitude after the living hell of a summer she had. She just needed to be alone with her own thoughts and try and heal emotionally. She kept on insisting to herself that she didn't need the professional help the abortion clinic suggested she get. Michele told the staff at the clinic everything they wanted to hear and said she knew of a wonderful woman named Mary Jane who was the best therapist you could ask for. Michele was convinced she could work it all out on her own, and on those hard days, she would get through them with little help from Mary Jane, something she had an endless supply of. She figured it would be like taking those little white pills she claimed to take only when she needed. She told herself *eventually, I won't even need that either*. Michele told Josh and Patty she would see them the following weekend. She wanted time to settle into her new surroundings. Michele had been distancing herself from them most of the summer, especially after telling Josh she didn't want to see him anymore. Michele was sitting in the very back row of the student union assembly hall, attending her last freshman orientation. She arrived just as the doors were shutting, and the orientation was starting. The speaker of the orientation had the students stand up and say their name, where they are from, and their major. Michele wasn't really paying much attention. She found this orientation very boring and really didn't care where most people were from no less who they were. One student introduced themselves, sending shock waves of panic tearing through her body. Michele, frozen with fear, listened to the towering young man who introduced himself by saying, "My name is Antonin Kofi Bedru Adama", in an accent Michele knew all too well. It was the accent the man with the robotic voice spoke with. An accent she will never forget and there was no mistaking it, the accent was the same. The first thing that ran through her mind was, *no this can't be, how did he find me!* Her stomach was in knots and the phantom pain of the abuse to her body returned. Michele could feel the acid rise from her stomach as the nausea started. Michele jumped out of her seat and ran out of the assembly hall, bolting through the exit doors trying to get outside of the building, hoping the fresh air would settle her stomach, but she was too late. She made it to the exit and was just outside of the door when her mouth filled with vomit. The acidic contents of her stomach spilled out of her mouth as Michele staggered around to the side of the building getting out of the public view. The contents of her stomach had emptied, and her breathing returned to normal. Michele started to calm herself, trying to understand that there was no way possible that the towering man with the accent was one of her rapists. The sheer terror of hearing that accent left doubt in her mind that it could be him. Michele never went to see Patty the following weekend. She stayed hidden in her dorm when she was not in class. The towering man with the accent was in two of her classes. She found him to be strange in a creepy sort of way.

He always sat up straight, eyes always locked onto the Professor as lectures were being given, and he never spoke unless he was spoken to. She described him to herself as being robot-like. No matter how hard she tried she just didn't feel safe outside of her dorm. She didn't know the towering man with the accent rented a cabin off campus or that her rapist with the accent was dead. If she had, maybe she would have felt a little safer and not isolate herself from the rest of the world. But that was the only way she knew how to protect herself; no one could hurt her if she stayed locked in her room. Towards the end of spring semester, after the 1985-1986 sporting season had ended, her roommate was around the dorm a little more often. She was quick to pick up on Michele's odd behavior. She noticed how uptight and guarded Michele was one Saturday so she asked Michele if she wanted to try something that would help loosen her up. Michele curiously asked what that something was. Michele's roommate pulled a small glass vial out of her desk. She walked over to Michele and sprinkled some of the white powder onto the back of her hand telling Michele to snort the white power up her nose. Michele snorted the cocaine. At first it burned her nose, then the drug kicked in with a high Michele grew especially fond of.

Josh and Patty had settled into college life rather well. Both were enjoying the newfound freedom of living away from home. Patty tried to get Michele to come over to Mercy for some parties and just to hang out, but didn't have much luck. Michele was either too busy, not interested, or had other plans. Josh didn't seem to care, he didn't want much to do with Michele after she broke up with him. Her not coming around was a relief for Josh. He didn't have to pretend to like Michele or that he didn't hate Michele for breaking up with him for no reason. He didn't have to pretend he wasn't angry or that he still wanted to be her friend. He was having a lot of fun getting high with Patty. It was the Columbus Day weekend of their freshman year Patty and Josh stayed on campus instead of going home for the long weekend. Their parents were running their church's retreat and recruiting weekend, an event that Josh and Patty wanted to stay as far away from as possible. The dorm was empty except for Josh and the third floor RA who he liked because he didn't care if Josh smoked pot in his room, as long a Campus Police didn't complain or do anything then the RA would look the other way and not bother anyone. Patty was hanging out in Josh's dorm room laying on his bed, chillin' while Josh sat at his desk packing a fresh bong. When Josh had finished, he joined Patty on his bed. Patty sat up, crossing her legs with her back to the foot of the bed, while Josh sat cross-legged with his back to the headboard. Josh told Patty he was going to shotgun her. Patty had no idea what the was, so Josh told her he was going to use the empty tube from a roll of paper towels to blow the smoke into her mouth. Patty, giggling at her own joke, said "Oh my gawd, that sounds totally tubular". She and Josh had gotten closer as friends since Patty got back from her trip and Michele broke up with him. They drew even closer this past month to the point where Patty would give Josh a hug every time, she saw him or a shoulder massage if he was sitting at his desk. She was cozying up to him from time to time. At this point they hadn't kissed nor had she told Josh how she felt about him. That didn't stop her from wearing a miniskirt with nothing underneath, and from seeing the grin on Josh's face, she knew it didn't go unnoticed. Josh lit the bong and took a big toke from it. After a few seconds of holding the smoke in his lungs, he put the empty role to his mouth and started exhaling as Patty put the other end to her mouth. Patty inhaled deeply. She loved the idea of taking in the smoke that came from inside Josh's lungs. After a moment, Patty exhaled and told Josh, "That was the most bitchin hit I have ever taken. Do it again." After the third time they shot gunned, Patty told Josh that she wanted him to do it without the tube and blow the smoke directly into her mouth. Josh liked that idea so after taking a hit off the bong, he leaned forward to blow the smoke into Patty's mouth. When Patty leaned forward, she put her hands on Josh's legs to balance herself. As their mouths connected, Patty inhaled Josh's breath till his lungs were empty. When he finished, he leaned back just enough so Patty could tilt her head back and exhale. While she was exhaling, Josh had placed his hands on her inner thighs. Patty tilted her head back down and found herself nose to nose with Josh. They just stared at one another as Josh gently massaged her inner thighs making his way up her skirt. Josh started kissing Patty as he continued to slide his hand all the way up her skirt, reaching around her with his other hand to unzip it. Patty wasted no time removing her top, then raised her hands to Josh's shoulders and pushed him back so she could straddle him. A completely naked Patty was staring down at Josh, savoring the moment, the moment she fantasized about since she found out in sex ed what a man's penis was used for. Josh had already slid his own pants off and started to slide himself into Patty who let out an audible moan of pleasure followed by an "OH GOD!" She let out a few more loud moans as Josh slid himself all the way in then grabbed her hips and flipped her over. As he started thrusting himself in her, Patty got lost in the sexual euphoria of finally having Josh inside her. In her state of ecstasy, she said the quiet part out loud, "Yes, finally he's in me, OH GOD he's finally in me!" It wasn't long before Patty started to climax. She wrapped her legs around Josh's waist and told him she was going to cum. Josh respond that he was too and was going to pull out. Patty squeezed her legs tighter around him and pulled him down locking her lips to his as she started to orgasm. Her orgasm was so intense Josh couldn't hold back as he started to orgasm with the woman he secretly wanted to be with. They were both lying back in bed cuddling staring up at the ceiling when Josh asked if this meant they were boyfriend and girlfriend now. Patty pulled him closer and started kissing him and Josh took that as a yes.

The summer after their freshman year was off to a good start, with Michele seeming to be back to her old self. It was the Michele that Josh and Patty knew. Even though it seemed like the old Michele was back, it didn't last long. Things quickly turned, and they saw a side of Michele they had not seen before. Michele had always been the ringleader of the trio, not out of fear, it was because Michele had a dominant personality compared to her laid-back just go- with-the-flow friends. Summer break quickly turned into a hellish summer with a cocaine fueled Michele and her undiagnosed bipolar personality now taking over and wreaking havoc more often than not. Josh and Patty were glad to be back at Mercy for the start of their sophomore year. Josh had invited the new roommate he was sharing a dorm room with this year to the annual keg party State and Mercy college had at the start of fall semester. Josh was glad to be away from Michele. He was relieved Michele didn't give him or Patty any trouble over them being girlfriend and boyfriend. Michele even said she didn't care if Patty wanted her sloppy seconds, she was done with Josh anyway. It was her bizarre behavior that was starting to scare Josh. Her mood was erratic. One minute she is happy go lucky and the next she was a total she devil, as he put it. Patty commented to Josh a few times on how volatile Michele had become, expressing concern for Michele. The week prior to their returning to campus from summer break, Michele had stopped calling them and once again isolated herself from her friends. The day of the keg party at Sandy Point beach, Michele called Patty and told her that she would pick both her and Josh up and they can ride with her to the keg party together. Patty, taking the offer as more of an order from Michele than an offer and, didn't argue she had become afraid of Michele and didn't dare say no. Whatever Michele wanted, Patty just went with it. She never knew how Michele would react especially after witnessing Michele going ballistic on the local diner's waitress that didn't bring Michele her order fast enough for her liking. The waitress had given them quick service, but Michele was "bouncing of the walls" so to speak, and was flying off the handle over the littlest things. This scared Patty to the point where she started to fear Michele. After Patty hung up the phone, she went to find Josh to tell him what was going on. Later that day at the Keg party, Michele spotted the new guy sitting at a picnic table with his back to her and was talking to the guy with the creepy accent.

Chapter 32

It was just after nine o'clock when the blond traveler woke up. She sat staring out through the windshield into the darkness of the swamp, her mind was dim and her senses dull from the alcohol, causing her to drift in and out of consciousness. Her head slumped forward with her forehead resting on the steering wheel she gently drifted off into the last few moments of sleep. She had fallen back to sleep long enough for the fog to clear from her mind when she woke up again. Now fully awake, she stared out into the tall sawgrass of the swampy Everglades. The air was as still as the night was black, and a quiet eeriness filled the swamp. Her nostrils filled with the rankness of the now dried urine that once soaked her clothing and car seat. With every breath she took, she remembered what happened earlier. She couldn't figure out if she should feel sorry for herself or be disgusted with herself. She did figure out that she had to clean herself up and change her clothing. She popped the latch for the front trunk of her Fiero before getting out of the car to get a change of clothes and a clean towel. Her mind was so focused on getting herself cleaned up, she didn't notice the heaviness, the stillness or the silence that surrounded her. Most nights, the swamp was alive with the nocturnal creatures that populated the Everglades. But tonight, this All Hallows Eve, it was as if the swap itself had died; there were no signs of life in any direction. The young woman stood next to the open door of her car and slid her soiled clothing off. Reaching into the car, she opened the glove box taking out several packets of wet wipes she had accumulated from the fast-food drive thrus, and the few bottles of water she had kept next to her on the passenger seat. Standing next to her car, she washed herself with the wet wipes and rinsed herself off with the bottled water. She managed to get herself cleaned up and dried off before putting on fresh clothes and wiping down the driver's seat. The black seat cover, with the neon-colored geometric shapes, absorbed almost all the urine. The Scotchgard fabric protector the dealership sprayed on the upholstery prevented the little urine that did soak through from being absorbed, making cleaning her seat easy. When she finished, she threw everything into the front trunk, as she closed the lid to the trunk, she noticed the silence that surrounded her. A chill ran down her spine as she looked out into the sheer black of the night, not being able to see beyond the light being emitted by her car's interior. No crickets were chirping and there was no rustling of the saw grass from the scurrying of the tiny creatures of the night, maneuvering in the safety and cover of the saw grass. There was just a deafening silence. She hurried back into her car. When she shut the door, the interior light went dark. The night was so dark she couldn't see the nose of her car. She looked up through the windshield, and she could see the sky, but no stars or moon were shedding their light. She felt like she was in an episode of The Twilight Zone. She started the car and turned on her headlights, hoping to see Evan's truck in the distance, praying she wasn't alone. There was nothing in front of her. She put the car's gear shifter in reverse using the backup lights to illuminate what was behind her, only to see more of nothing. At that moment, she wanted nothing more than to just get the hell out of there and back to the main road. She sat there taking in her immediate surroundings of the interior of her car. Looking around, the first thing she saw was the open bag with the half-consumed bottle of vodka, the little vials of cocaine, and the sleeping pills she bought, hoping they would grant her a good night's sleep free of the dreams that haunted her, scattered on the bottom of the bag. She looked past the bag and saw her notepad. Picking it up, she started to read what she wrote. After reading what she wrote, she continued her search till she found the handgun and retrieved it from its resting place. She tried squeezing the trigger and cocking the hammer to get the gun to work. When she had no luck with that, she tried to flip open the barrel, but even the barrel was frozen shut. Sitting there in the dark, she knew what she wanted and that was for the night terrors to stop. That wasn't the only thing, she wanted the past few years of her life erased from her memory as if it never happened. She wanted to go back home, where daddy was her hero and protected her from all the bad in the world. Back to when she had friends who loved her, she wanted her father to take back those harsh words he said after she hung up the phone just a few months ago. She thought that Daddy knew none of it was her fault. None of it would have happened if he had come crashing in like Superman or at least the Superman hero she thought he was. She knew that none of that was going to happen. Now he was the monster who said he was ashamed of what she had become and the ignoble child he never intended to raise. Convinced that the only way she could bring her mental suffering to an end, the only way she could find the peace she desperately sought, was to shut her eyes, go to sleep, and never open them again. She knew what she had to do, but not here, not in the swamp. She wanted to sit on a white sandy beach and watch the sunrise for a final time. She wanted one last sunrise, one last ray of light, one last breath of the ocean air before slipping off into the darkness of death in hopes of finding the peace she longed for. The peace of being freed from her tortured mind. She sat peering through the windshield looking out into the area of sawgrass that was being illuminated by her headlights, looking for the answers that wouldn't come. The thought that did enter her mind was, *is there enough vodka and sleeping pills left to get the job done?* She thought that maybe after taking the sleeping pills and drinking the last of the vodka, she would wade out into the ocean and let the tide take her body away. She had close to a three-hour drive to get across Alligator Alley and find her way onto the beach. It was getting late, and she didn't want to fall asleep at the wheel, nor did she want to do the drive in the daylight which would mean she would need to find a motel or stay where she was, waiting for the following night. Neither option worked for her; she wanted to end this now. No more sleep, no more night terrors. She reached into her bag where she had just the thing and plenty of it to keep her awake. She unscrewed the cap to one of the vials that contained cocaine and dumped its contents on the back of her fist and began to snort the white powder. She threw the empty vial onto the floor of the passenger side and started to slowly back her car down the narrow dirt road. The narrow road and swampy surroundings didn't provide a spot for her to turn around, she had to back her car up all the way to the main road. She backed onto the main road with her car pointed East, which was the direction she wanted to go. Sitting with her car idling on the side of the main road, she had become frustrated because she wasn't feeling the effects of the white powder. Reaching into her bag she pulled out another vial and repeated the process, tilting her back and snorting of snorting its contents. She rested her head on the headrest, waiting for the second dose to kick in. It didn't take long for the drug to do its thing. In a matter of seconds, the white powder did its job. The young woman was wired. Dropping the car into gear and hammering the gas pedal, she sped off towards Miami. She was cruising at 100 mph. The V6 engine in the Formula model of the 1987 Pontiac Fiero made it easy for drivers of a light car like the Fiero to achieve and cruise at high rates of speed. Alligator Alley is a desolate road during the day and generally deserted at night. The Florida Highway Patrol would set their speed traps during the day, making it easier for her to cruise at the high speed she was going. She was twenty minutes into her drive and feeling the full effects of the cocaine when out of nowhere, and at a rate of speed that seemed to match the speed of the Fiero, an alligator darted out in front of her, shooting out from the tall sawgrass on the left side of the road. The gator was making its way to the canal that flowed into the pond on the right side of the road. Quickly jerking the steering wheel to avoid hitting the reptilian swamp monster sent the Fiero out of control. The high rate of speed, the sudden jerking of the wheel, and a driver fueled by cocaine were the perfect storm for disaster. The car's left front tire hit the alligator causing the speeding car to roll over several times, the high rate of speed she was traveling at caused enough momentum for the red 1987 Pontiac Fiero, and driver to go airborne, sending its exterior car parts sprawling all over the road before crashing into the pond. The car splashed into the water on its roof, floating with its wheels still spinning before it started to sink. The rolling motion of the car whipped the driver from side to side smashing her head into the driver's side window and knocking her unconscious. The young female driver was suspended upside down, and the car was taking on water as it started to submerge in the black murky waters of the Everglades. The woman in white, standing on the edge of the sawgrass that surround the bank of the pond was accompanied by two shadowy figures. They watched as the car was swallowed up by the swamp, sinking into the depths of the swampy grave, never to be recovered. As the taillights sank below the surface of the water, the young female's head emerged from the water, gasping for air. She managed to roll onto her back and float face-up, gasping for air and trying to get the water out of her lungs. She lay floating in the center of the pond above the spot where she came crashing in, crying and sobbing, "Oh god what was I thinking? I don't want to die! Please daddy help me! HELP ME DADDY HELP ME!" Her screaming was distracting her from the apex predator that was stalking her and waiting for the right moment before snatching its evening meal. The hungry alligator raised its head out of the water just inches from her. The silent predator was sizing up his victim before clamping its jaws down on the midsection of the young, terrified woman floating on her back in front of him calling out for her daddy to save her. With a swish of its powerful tale the gator propelled himself forward, opened his jaws, and clamped down on the young woman. Her arms beat down on the top of the gator's head and her legs kicked wildly. She tried in vain to free herself before she was dragged into the death roll. There was a loud shout from the edge of the small pond near the spot the canal drained into the pond "Big Al isn't going to eat you." She recognized that voice. It was the voice of the man in the Chevy K10 pickup truck. Evan Mills stepped out from the tall sawgrass to reveal himself. "Bring her over here Big Al." The gator, doing as he was instructed, brought the young woman over to him. Big Al climbed out of the pond, opened his jaws, and set the young woman down before backing himself into the pond. Evan said, "Thanks buddy" as he reached down and offered a helping hand to the young woman telling her, "Trust me you're not hurt." and helped her up. The young woman looked at Even with bewilderment as she had no words for him or for what just happened. Evan smiled at her and said, "I'll explain" He began the story by telling the young woman about the first day on the new job and how he came to meet Big Al "I was busy unloading my equipment to collect my usual water samples when I heard thrashing on the banks of the swamp. I went to investigate and saw that Big Al had gotten tangled up in an old poacher's trap." He told her how he went down the bank to free the gator from the trap. "With all the thrashing Big Al was doing, I lost my balance and fell forward just as Big Al broke free. Big Al latched down on my arm and dragged me into the water and into the death roll." The young woman turned and looked out onto the pond at the last of the air bubbles coming from her car and said," Am I dead too? Is my body still in the car?" Evan replied with a soft and gentle, "Yes", as he gave her a few moments to get a grasp of the situation. She sighed heavily before asking Evan if he was there to take her to heaven. In that same soft and gentle tone, he told her, "I am not here to take you to heaven, I am here to take you somewhere else." The words "somewhere else" petrified her. She started crying and begging him not to take her to hell, that she was sorry, and she pleaded for forgiveness. Evan assured her he wasn't there to take her to hell. He was there to take her to a place where her consciousness is reborn. Her consciousness would flow into her new life much like a flame that passes from one candle to another. It is her soul's journey to break the cycle of life and death by working to achieve enlightenment and liberation. Her rebirth into her next life's journey will be influenced by the karmic imprints of her actions from this life. He held out his arms so he could take her by the hands, telling her it's time to go. Evan guided her into the warm glowing light that grew around him.

As the light began to fade, the woman in white slowly turned to Sabastian and Kathleen Gibson and spoke. "You deserved to know what happened to your daughter and why you never heard from her after she stormed out of the house all those years ago." Tears were rolling down the sides of Sabastion's face, with the regret he felt for saying what he said to Michele. "It was my fault that she said those cruel words to Paige" as he referred to the phone call Michele made to Paige on the morning of August 14th, 1987. Michele had hung up the phone and turned to her father, telling him, "I won daddy I beat Paige and his lawyer at their own game. I won, aren't you proud of me daddy?" Sabastian was furious at what he overheard from the phone call, telling Paige it wasn't a real baby, then hearing Michele say, "I won daddy," sent him over the edge. He screamed, "Only a monster would do such an unholy thing." His voice was rising with every word that he spoke, his face distorted from a scowl, he pointed a finger at Michele hollering, "No daughter of mine would ever be that evil and say those cruel things nor commit such heinous act!" He told her it went against her catholic upbringing and everything he and her mother stood for. Sabastian never saw the monster that he created. It was that phone call that showed him that he created the monster standing there next to the phone. He was the reason why Michele turned out the way she did. He wanted a chance to tell Michele he was sorry he wasn't lashing out at her; he was lashing out at himself. He was angry at his failure to do right by his daughter, even if it meant she was mad at him for saying no. Instead, he gave in to her every whim. He had raised a daughter who knew no boundaries and feared no consequences. Kathleen stood silent, filled with her own regret, as she watched her husband weep. She was unable to say out loud the thing that had tormented her for so many years. The thoughts that said, "What if I told my daughter about my past and my mistakes? What if I just admitted the truth that my daughter was just like me?" Burying her face in her husband's arm, hiding her shame, Kathleen began sobbing. She was filled with her own regrets of failure. The woman in white gave Sabastian and Kathleen the time they needed before following Evan and Michele and guiding them into the fading light so they too could break the karmic cycle they were in.

On the opposite bank, the three shadowy figures who kept watch from the sawgrass on the dirt road, and kept watch from the sand dunes in Cancun stood watching the red 1987 Pontiac Fiero that contained the earthly shell of Michele Gibson slowly sink into the muddy bottom of the Everglades.

www.ingramcontent.com/pod-product-compliance
Lightning Source LLC
Chambersburg PA
CBHW021802130726

47987CB00008B/2987